ET AUGMENTED REALITY CHANGE HOW YOU READ A BOOK

With your smartphone, iPad or tablet you can use the **Neighbur Vue** app to invoke the augmented reality experience to literally read outside the book.

neighbur

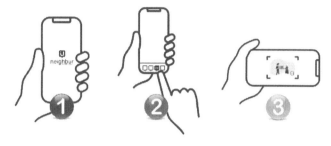

1. Notice the spelling: download the free Neighbur Vue app from the Apple App Store or Google Play

2. Open and select the [vue] (vue) option

3. Point your camera lens at the full image with the [vue] and enjoy the augmented reality experience.

Go ahead and try it right now with the cover of this book.

Once the content begins, click the 'Lock' icon to lock the content onto your phone.

ENDORSEMENTS

"*I love reading fiction, and when I read Janet-Lynn's book I was certainly taken on a journey. She is an author with a powerful imagination and her beautiful writing skills are very much highlighted in* **Forever is Today**. *I couldn't put the book down! A MUST READ!*"

Judy O'Beirn
President and Founder of
Hasmark Publishing International
International Best-Selling Author of
Unwavering Strength Series

"*The characters of this story grabbed me immediately. Get engaged in this imaginable story and feel the familiarity of the places and events.*"

Ann Collins
International Best-Selling Author
of *Hope Loss enCourage*

"*A hard-hitting, emotion-driven narrative that takes the reader by the hand and walks them through a story piled full of family, growing pains and love. Janet-Lynn Morrison's story aims directly for the heart and succeeds in presenting the reader with a beautifully moving and heartfelt story.*"

Katia Stern
International Best-Selling Author of
You Were Born WOW

"As a fiction writer, I am always looking for a great storyteller. Janet-Lynn has the power to transport her audience and each chapter jolts the reader into a cacophony of pure imagination. Her writing is heart-wrenching, subtle and profound, all the while taking you on a literary escapade of immaculate storytelling. **Forever is Today** is a must read! This book reminds me of a movie. I can't wait to see what else this author has in store for us. She is MAGIC!"

Pashmina P.
International Best-Selling Author of *The Cappuccino Chronicles Trilogy* and *What is A Gupsey?*

"*Forever Is Today* is truly gripping… Right from the beginning all the way to the end. And, the ending!! Wow, never saw that coming. Well done!"

Peggy McColl,
New York Times Best-Selling Author

FOREVER
is Today

By
Janet-Lynn Morrison

Published by
Hasmark Publishing
www.hasmarkpublishing.com

Permission should be addressed in writing to Janet-Lynn Morrison at
jl@janet-lynn.com

Editor: Kathryn Young
kathryn@hasmarkpublishing.com
Cover & Book Design: Anne Karklins
anne@hasmarkpublishing.com
Cover photography: Peter Dušek Photography
peter@peterdusek.com

ISBN 13: 978-1-989756-57-7
ISBN 10: 1989756573

DEDICATION

I dedicate this book to my daughters—Cassidy, Madeline, and Eve—who are the source of my single greatest inspiration and without whom this book would never exist. Each day, my love for you three girls inspires me to follow my dreams and to *live impossibly* in hopes that you will one day reach your impossible.

ACKNOWLEDGMENTS

Life, for me, is about making our dreams become a reality. A lot of that has to do with the people we surround ourselves with who share in our vision, who subscribe to a similar purpose, and who support us while we step out into the unknown and beyond.

I have been fortunate to have had people in my life who touched me in ways that invigorated my desire to succeed. They have helped me become the person I am, a person who lives by the personalized slogan, *live impossibly*. They will always play an important role in my life, and I will be forever grateful for their presence and influence.

I am so fortunate in my life to be surrounded by such a wonderful family. My special thanks go to *Jeff* for always supporting my myriad ideas no matter how crazy and for being such a great listener and shoulder to lean on, always.

Thanks to my eldest daughter, *Cassidy*, my creative editor, whom I couldn't have done this project without. You have more talent in your pinky finger than most of us have in our lifetimes. Remember to decide and then do it; you can accomplish anything.

Thanks to my second daughter, *Madeline*, who has inspired me every day. Since your diagnosis of autoimmune hepatitis, your daily courage gives me the determination to be the best mother. Thank you for allowing me to share many of the personal details of your life with the world.

Thanks to my youngest daughter, *Eve*, my sweet girl, who always lights up my day and who gave me some wonderful ideas for the love story. You are a true romantic at heart.

Thanks to *Tim*, the best brother a girl could have. You have always been my most cherished confidant in this thing called life. You are the kindest and most giving person I know, and I will love you forever!

Thanks to *Sondra*, a wonderful sister-in-law. I am so thankful my brother found such a worthy partner to travel through life with. You are strong and intelligent and keep smiling no matter what. Together you have raised three amazing children—Alice, Quinn, and Hannah Burton. I love you all.

Thanks to my in-laws—*Sue, Gord*, and *Jennifer Morrison*—for everything you do and for being three incredible role models who have always demonstrated what parents should be and what family is all about. My love to Isiah and Avery—two amazing kids.

Thanks to a special friend to our family, *Mohit Arora*, who we met at a Liver Stroll event in 2018 in Toronto. He was among the speakers, as was Maddy. He hit it off with each of us on a different level, so much so that we remained in touch. Mohit is an incredibly strong, compassionate man who was a liver transplant recipient as a teenager in 1993. He helped me to understand some of the emotional repercussions of this experience. We look forward to a lifetime of amazing conversation and laughs. I will be thinking of your special day when my book launches.

My family would like to thank all the amazing and dedicated individuals who make The Hospital for Sick Kids in Toronto one of the best in the world. The kindness and professionalism on all levels of care have been very meaningful to our family, and we are so very grateful.

Thanks to *Dr. Simon Ling* (Sick Kids Hospital), *Dr. Jordan Feld* MD, MPH (Toronto General Hospital), *Dr. Gideon Hirschfield* (Toronto General Hospital), for your ongoing support, guidance, and expertise in the treatment of autoimmune liver disease.

Thanks to *Steve Mendoza*, my business partner and friend, for your ongoing support, excitement, interest, and love of reading and learning. You helped me to develop the story chapter by chapter by listening and allowing me to share my ideas. You also helped me to be creative during a time when much of the world was spinning out of control with fear due to COVID-19. I will never forget when you said, "I wish your parents were here to see their little girl becoming an inspirational woman!" That meant more to me than you could ever know.

Thanks to *Peter Noce* for being my technology genius and for being so generous with his gift of time. Thanks to *Peter Dusek* for capturing the perfect picture for the cover of the book and for creating the perfect website.

Thanks to *Peter and Tess Harvie*. I never imagined becoming fast friends and besties with an eighty-six-year-old gentleman. Peter and Tess are not only characters in my book—they are real people. I miss Peter terribly as, after a two-year friendship, I had to let him go from this world. I was honored to have been by his side, and his amazing wife Tess gifted me with the most gorgeous keepsake ring as a treasured memory. My time with Peter was full of laughter and tears, mostly from laughing at his bad jokes. We watched movies, played catch and darts, and exercised. We also spent countless hours walking around the large pond at the back of his residence feeding the ducks and sharing life stories. I love you both, and even though our friendship was short, Peter, it will last as long as I live. I stay in touch with Tess to this day, and she is, as always, a force to be reckoned with. I've never met such a strong and determined woman, and she is a true lady through and through. There are no words for the admiration I feel for her.

Thanks to *Bob and Linda Proctor*. If it weren't for Bob Proctor's coaching course, who knows where I'd be today. This experience led to an introduction to Linda, who shared with Bob a piece of my writing, to which he said, "That woman needs to get in touch with Peggy McColl." Of course, that's exactly what I did, and only a few short months later, I completed the manuscript of *Forever is Today*. It is truly amazing what you can accomplish once you simply decide.

Thanks to *Hasmark Publishing International*. If you want to know what having a dynamic and professional team backing your project feels like, ask me, and I will let you know how wonderful it is to belong to this book family. Better yet, write your own book and join us! My gratitude is overflowing for everyone on the team, especially to Judy. A special thank you also to my fantastic editor, whose insights and suggestions were the icing on the cake. I will strive to become the highest example of a grateful author as I share my books with the world. As John Kennedy said: *As we*

*express our gratitude, we must never forget that the highest apprecia-
tion is not to utter words but to live by them.*

Thanks to *Peggy McColl* and *Phil Goldfine*. Thank you, Peggy,
for the wonderful endorsement and for believing in this project
to the extent that you put your reputation on the line by sharing
my story with Phil, one of the most celebrated producers in Hol-
lywood, to be shopped for the big screen.

TABLE OF CONTENTS

PROLOGUE

From as far back as I can remember, I've loved words and the way no other art form expresses an idea quite the same. Words create worlds within your mind, they pull emotions from within you, and they make you think about what you have just read for days, weeks, or a lifetime.

When you master words and the ability to weave them together just so, you become a creator. You create a world that starts with one silent idea inside your mind, which then expands into people, with friends, families, and interests. And then you give them a story of their own. The goal is always to share your work, get it published, and when you do, you will have succeeded at creating an entire universe that becomes alive in the minds of millions.

I have spent my whole life thinking about what makes a work of written words important and memorable. I have come to believe that the works that have stood the test of time all shared a common goal—to make one experience a range of emotions. The beauty of words is like no other form of art in that writing can richly capture a person's deepest desire, pain, fear, or joy. Other kinds of artwork can only suggest these emotions.

Writers enjoy a certain extra freedom when creating. We are not bound by a limited number of notes to form a melody like musicians. We do not have to make do with the existing world like photographers. And I think that our literary masterpieces are better understood than the works of visual artists, who have to leave their work to the viewer's own imagination.

With the ability to use almost limitless combinations of words, I like to think writers have "more brushes and more colors of paint" than any artist. We can create images with colors that do not exist, while our characters are free to develop into exactly who they want to be.

On a special night of the year, where words are celebrated at an event in New York City, I found myself for the first time without any words. With a glass of champagne in one hand and feeling short of breath no matter how much I loosened my tie, I knew this night would change my and my family's lives forever.

I watched the evening commencing as people made their way to their tables, and the opening jazz musicians packed up their instruments. I made my way to my table, greeting some of the individuals being honored who were sitting with me. With a smile in my heart, I waited for the event to start. After the guests were seated, everyone hushed as our host for the evening walked up on stage. He reached the podium and spoke into the microphone.

"Welcome to the Annual Fiction Writers of America Awards!"

CHAPTER ONE

September 13

I miss the beach and the ocean. This has been a long trip, and I never thought I'd say this, but I'm tired of fast food and hotels. We are arriving at our new home in New York today. I can't wait to get out of this car and explore.

As I looked out the window at the unfamiliar houses and vegetation, I felt a sense of uncertainty. Picking up your entire life and moving across the country was not the easiest thing to do in your senior year of high school. I had nearly convinced my parents to let me stay in California with one of my friends until high school was over, and then I would start my first year at Stanford. *Nearly* meant they did not go for it at all. While I was still seventeen with limited funds of my own, it looked like I was going along for the ride until graduation.

I would have to make new friends, start on a new soccer team with new teammates, and endure my first east coast winter. While I had been the best offense on my old team, I'd always been a bit of a loner in my own time. I didn't mind it this way, much preferring to spend my time reading and writing. I wanted to be a famous author one day, and I liked to pull my inspiration from observing the people around me. This was why I kept a journal where I could write any interesting occurrences that happened in my day-to-day life.

New York State was not at all like my hometown in California. I had lived in San Diego my whole life, where it was dry and hot, and I lived two blocks away from the best Mexican restaurant in the city. I was pretty sure people here put ground beef instead of flank steak in their tacos and would not be able to stomach a hot chili pepper contest.

I sat in the backseat of my parents' SUV with my twin sister Anna. She was looking out her side of the car, and I could hear some corny love ballad coming from her headphones.

I poked her shoulder as I saw our new town's welcome sign. She smiled at me, and we looked out my window at the sign that read, "Welcome to Saratoga Springs." Old brick buildings and manicured gardens made up the scenery of our new home. Friendly looking people walked around shopping and drinking coffee in the ease of late afternoon on a Saturday.

Within a few minutes, we pulled up to a large stone home with black French windows and a solarium on the second floor. This was our new house, which Anna and I had only seen in photos and on a FaceTime call with our parents when they first came to look at it.

We were on a quiet road where the houses were far apart. There may have been no palm trees in sight, but everything was green and lush. San Diego was too dry to have grass this healthy and vibrant, and there were apple trees in the front yard. We had five acres of land, most of which backed onto a forest. I had to admit that it was beautiful here. Everything was different than I was used to. From brown to green, stucco to brick, and condensed to sprawling amounts of space.

"We're here," my mother, Elizabeth, said melodically. We all got out of the car and looked around. The moving truck would be here the next day, but we still had our essentials in the trailer attached to the car, and much of our new furniture was already inside from my parents' last visit.

"What do you guys think?" my father, Rick, asked.

"It's beautiful," Anna said, smiling up at the house.

"Definitely not San Diego," I said.

"That it isn't," my dad said. "But it's a new adventure, and we're only two hours from New York City, so that means we'll get to try Wahlburgers!"

"Sorry, Dad, I don't think it will compare to In-N-Out," Anna said definitively.

"Well, you never know, you guys, you might find you like east coast living even better than west coast," Dad said.

"Like you said, dear, it's a new adventure!" my mom added.

After bringing in our luggage, dipping my feet in the pool, and taking a quick look around, I felt I needed to expend some energy after the long, cross-country road trip. I grabbed my skateboard from the trunk of our SUV and went down the quiet road.

I rode along the side of the road and breathed in the fresh air. The gentle end of summer breeze had the smell of fresh-cut grass and burgers cooking on the neighbors' grills. I had to admit, starting over somewhere new could be cool. New experiences and new people would surely bring some interesting writing material.

I saw a paved trail coming up on my right and leaned to guide my skateboard in its direction. I glanced back at my new house with a smile, and as I turned the corner into the hood of trees, I hit a rough patch of cement and completely wiped out. I went down onto the ground, my hands scraping the pavement and my board flying into the tall grass.

"Oh, my God! Are you okay?" a girl's voice called from the trail. I lay sprawled on the concrete, looking up into the sky until the girl reached me, and the blue was obstructed by her wild golden hair.

"Uh, yeah, I'm good," I said, trying to brush it off like it was not totally humiliating to have someone witness my spill. I began to stand up, brushing the stones from my hands onto my shorts. When I stood, I looked at the girl. I had clearly interrupted her run, judging from the headphones and workout clothes she wore. She was slim and small, with a soft expression, bright blue eyes, and sun-kissed skin.

"Are you sure?" She stared at the blood on my hands. "Can I get you like a bandage or something?" She could not help but grin as she spoke, and an embarrassed smile grew on my own face. We both laughed.

"No, I'm good," I said.

"Are you new around here?"

"Is it that obvious?"

"I just come this way at this time every day, and I always see the same people."

"Yeah, I just moved in up the road," I said, pointing to my house.

"Huh," she said, still slightly out of breath from her run. "That's me right there." She pointed to an even closer bungalow style home with four cars in the driveway.

I could not help but notice she was incredibly beautiful. Her features were so soft and pretty, making me almost mad at her for having to be the one to witness my wipeout. Still, I had the privilege of meeting her, regardless of the way it happened.

"I'm Joel," I said, extending my bloody hand. She scrunched up her face and laughed, making me feel like an idiot again. Still, she took my wrist with her hand and shook it.

"I'm Bea," she said. "Short for Beatrice. My parents suck at names."

She looked down into the grass and plucked a small yellow buttercup from the ground. She handed it to me. "Welcome to the neighborhood, Joel."

I smiled and took the tiny flower. "Thank you."

"I have to get home, but feel free to come say hey. I have a brother too."

"Okay, yeah," I said. "I will."

"Okay." She grinned again. "Get home safe."

"You too." I laughed.

I watched her break into a run and head down the road.

When I got home, Billy Holiday was playing through the rooms, and the smell of Chinese food came from the kitchen. My dad was unwrapping our new white and blue dishes from a box and putting them away in the chocolate brown over-head cupboards. The large kitchen had a huge island, granite countertops and floors, and a wine chiller with a glass door. I came in and grabbed an egg roll from one of the takeout boxes.

"Hey Joel," my dad said when he noticed me. "How'd the exploring go?"

"Pretty good. Looks like a nice neighborhood."

"Yeah, it is! Grab some dinner and start unpacking your room. Most of your boxes are up there."

I made a plate with fried rice and sweet and sour chicken and went into the living room. Anna and my mom sat on the hardwood floors with photo albums scattered around them. My mom was very sentimental and kept every picture ever taken of us. She would become panicked at family gatherings, always intent on capturing every moment. They were laughing at something in one of the albums when they looked up to see me.

"Why are you smiling like an idiot?" Anna said with a raised eyebrow.

"I'm not," I said defensively. I quickly wiped the grin off my face to replace it with a serious glare at my sister.

"You were," she said back.

"Whatever, I'm going to start unpacking in my room."

"Okay, sweetie," my mom said, getting up to put the photo album on the shelf next to the fireplace. "Bring the plate back when you're done."

In my room, there were a lot of boxes and a new bed and desk. My parents had sold most of our furniture out west, and we had all agreed it would be easier to just replace it. My backpack was sitting on my mattress, and I went to find my journal. I pulled it out and took the pen from its spine. On a fresh page, I wrote one word: *Bea*. In our brief encounter, she had made an impression on me. I could still picture her face an hour later. I thought she would make an interesting subject to base a character on. I quickly jotted down some notes on our first meeting. Then I shoveled in a few bites of food, grabbed a hoodie, and headed back downstairs. "Guys, I'm going out," I called to my family as I put on my shoes.

"Where are you going?" my mom asked as she appeared in the foyer.

"I met a neighbor earlier, and she invited me over. She's got a brother too."

"Okay, well, don't be too late," my mom said.

"I won't," I replied and went out the door.

I stood outside the large wooden double doors to Bea's home, aware that my palms were sweaty, and my heart was racing. I heard once that your body couldn't tell the difference between being nervous and excited. Since there isn't anything too nerve-racking about meeting some new neighbors, it must be the excitement of seeing a certain set of blue eyes that was causing my anxiety.

I smiled inwardly and knocked on the heavy ornate door.

A woman who was the older version of Bea opened the door. "Hello! Can I help you?" she asked in a friendly voice.

"Hi." I completely lost all my talent with words at that moment. "Err, your daughter ran into me earlier, well actually I fell on my own, but she said to come over. Ummm, I just moved here, and I...."

"You must be Joel," the woman said with a laugh, saving me from my own rambling. "Come on in. Bea and her brother are in the kitchen. You're welcome to stay for dinner."

"Thanks," I said gratefully as I stepped inside. The house smelled deliciously of chicken and mushrooms, while the décor was kind of quirky and artistic. Many paintings and odd sculptures scattered the main room, and on the far wall was a huge bookshelf filled with the multi-colored spines of vintage books. I would have to check those out later.

"I'm Bea's mom. You can call me Ria," the woman said and then asked me if I wouldn't mind leaving my shoes by the door. I kicked my Vans off and placed them neatly to the side.

"Follow me, dear," Ria said, walking into the large open concept living space.

She led me into the kitchen, where a tall blonde boy who looked about my age was stirring something in a sizzling pan. "Hey guys, we have company tonight," Ria said.

The boy looked up from what he was doing, and a curly blonde mop of hair popped up from behind the island. Bea stood up and smiled. "Hey, Joel! Couldn't wait to see me again, eh?"

"Uh," I said with a laugh, feeling a little uncomfortable.

"This is my brother Jeremy."

"Hey man, Bea told me you wiped out pretty hard today," Jeremy said, leaning against the counter and crossing his arms, a spatula in one hand.

"Umm, yes," I said, looking back to Bea. She did not look a tad bit apologetic that she had already shared my humiliation with her entire family. Instead, she just smiled with an absent-minded look on her face.

"Yeah, one time I wiped out on that trail on my bike and broke my arm," Jeremy offered, maybe noticing my red face. "So, you just moved here? Will you be going to Saratoga Springs Secondary?"

"Yeah, I start Monday."

"Where'd you move from, dear?" Ria asked from her perch on one of the island barstools.

"I'm from San Diego," I answered with a nod.

"Wow, you're a Cali boy," Ria said with raised eyebrows. "Must be why you left an impression on my daughter."

"I actually didn't know that. What brings you to Saratoga Springs?" Bea asked.

"Well, my dad is an engineer, and he got a new job in New York. But my mom hates the city, so we moved here. It was their compromise, as they say. My mom still gets to have a big house and yard, and my dad got his new BMW for the commute."

My three hosts all laughed. "Sounds like a fair deal," Ria said. "Jer, when will dinner be ready?"

"Two minutes, Mom," Jeremy said, turning back to his mushrooms.

"Perfect," Ria said. "Joel, the glasses are in the cabinet to your left, and there are soda and juice in the fridge. Don't hesitate to help yourself to whatever when you're here. Just make yourself at home."

"Thanks," I said. I stole a glance at Bea, who was tossing the contents of a large salad. Her hair bounced, and she was humming softly, so I could just barely hear her. I recognized the melody as a classic ACDC song.

"Hey guys, almost ready?" A man came in and put his hand on Ria's shoulder.

"Almost!" Bea said. "Dad, this is Joel. He just moved in down the road, and he's staying for dinner. Joel, this is my dad, Brandon."

I went to shake his hand. "Hi, sir, nice to meet you."

Brandon took my hand and shook it firmly. "Likewise. Where'd you move from?"

"San Diego," I answered.

"That's quite a change," he said, going back to his wife's side.

"Alright, and we're all set," Jeremy said, piling his mushrooms into a serving bowl.

"Great!" Ria said, standing up. "Joel, grab that bowl there if you don't mind."

I obediently grabbed the bowl of bread rolls closest to me and followed my new neighbors into their dining room.

We sat in front of a huge feast of salad, fresh rolls, juicy chicken, and the best mushrooms I have ever had. Bea and her family were very close, I could tell. You could feel the warmth they had toward each other just from being around them.

Jeremy would throw a piece of cucumber at Bea, and she would lick it and put it back in his salad. And Brandon would lovingly take his wife's hand or pour her more wine, smiling at her as if it were their first date.

"So, Joel," Brandon said as we ate. "What sort of interests do you have?"

"I'm a writer, sir," I said, stealing a glance at Bea as she watched me. "I've always loved books and literature."

"That's excellent," Brandon said, impressed. "You know that our Skidmore University has an excellent creative writing department."

"I didn't know that," I said.

"Yes, it's one of the best schools in the state," Brandon said with pride.

"Dad's an English Lit professor at Skidmore," Jeremy piped up.

"Wow, that's great, sir," I said. "I'll have to check out the campus."

"I can most definitely introduce you to the right people if you're applying in the spring. Jeremy's in his first year."

"And he has the best off-campus housing money can buy," Ria said to me with a wink.

"I'm an American Studies major," Jeremy said. "It is a great school, lots of interesting classes, lots of hot foreign girls. They're always more fun when they're—"

"Alright, Jeremy," Ria said, shaking her head.

"I was going to say studying," Jeremy said, grinning at me.

"You've never even looked at a girl who can read, let alone study," Bea said, looking down at her food. They all laughed, except for Jeremy, who glared at his sister, but not without affection.

I helped clear the table and clean up the kitchen after dinner. Ria kept saying "such a gentleman," as I did as much as I could to eliminate the mess. When everything was put away, I wandered into the living room. Bea was standing at the towering book-shelves along the far wall. I came up to stand next to her.

"It's my dad's collection of first editions," she said. I looked back at the books, only to realize their significance and value. Names like Jane Austen, Thomas Hardy, and Mark Twain littered the shelves. All were in pristine condition and alphabetized by the last name from A to Z. I was taken aback; I think I even gasped a little. Bea must have noticed because she spoke.

"He's collected them since before I was born. He used to read *Huckleberry Finn* and *Alice in Wonderland* to me when I was a kid, right out of the first editions."

"These are incredible," I said, truly astounded. "So, you like reading too?"

"I do," Bea said, smiling, seemingly with fond memories playing behind her eyes. "I always had my nose in a book growing up. I did not have many friends. Kids can be mean." She shrugged as if to say, but what can you do. "My best friends were The Hardy Boys, Peter Pan, and Nancy Drew."

"Mine were Holden Caulfield and Jim Hawkins," I said.

"I loved *Catcher in the Rye* and *Treasure Island* too," she said, looking up at me.

Brandon, Ria, and Jeremy joined us in the living room. Ria perched herself elegantly on the armchair, her wine glass in hand, while Jeremy sprawled out on the couch. Brandon walked up to the shelves on the opposite side from where I stood.

"What was your favorite?" Brandon asked, searching his shelves.

"Definitely *Treasure Island*," I said. "It's an epic tale of adventure and the ultimate pirate story."

Brandon plucked a small and frail brown book out of his collection. He smiled down at it and handed it to me. "Take it, so you can enjoy the story as it was first meant to be experienced."

I hesitated, my eyes bulging at this generous offer. "Sir, I couldn't."

"Truthfully, it's in rough condition, which significantly lessens the value," he said, still holding out the book. "And I have other copies."

Carefully I took the book from his hand and stared at it. "Thank you," I said, so enamored by this little book and my new neighbor's generosity.

I held it close to my chest and smiled at my new friends. I looked at Bea. She was looking back, her eyes sparkling, her fingers playing with a strand of blonde hair.

September 13 (later)

I met a girl today whose eyes challenge the blue of the ocean. They could replace it altogether. The beauty of the ocean has a new name for me. Bea.

CHAPTER TWO

---◦◦◇◦◦---

I woke up, and my first thought was of Bea. The excitement I was experiencing reminded me of Christmas mornings when I would meet Anna in the hallway and race downstairs to see the magical sight of gifts surrounding our Christmas tree. After only a few waking moments, I decided that I had to figure out a way to see this girl today. I jumped out of bed and rummaged through a box until I found my shower kit. I headed into my and Anna's bathroom, turned on the hot water, and took a quick shower.

I headed downstairs to see if anyone else was up. Halfway down the stairs, I could smell the fresh coffee and followed my nose to the kitchen, where my mother sat on the window seat overlooking the front yard. She held her favorite rose painted mug that my sister had given her for Mother's Day the previous year while listening to classical piano music that played softly from the portable speaker.

"Morning," she said cheerfully as I came into the room. I could always count on Mom being up and ready with a warm smile to greet me at the start of the day, no matter what was going on in life. Glass half full? Rose-colored glasses? I did not know how she did it day after day, but she never spoke in negative terms or ever sounded fearful. Here we were, moving and starting all over, far from friends or familiarity. She left her book club of twelve years, and instead of being sad, she is excited to start one of her own. All her favorite restaurants and shops have been left behind. "I'll just have to find some new ones," she had said.

I recalled my interactions with Bea's mom last evening and wondered if Bea was more like her mother or her father.

I still felt warm from the interactions from the night before. I was excited to get to know this family better. Jeremy seemed cool, and I thought maybe we'd become friends if he didn't care that I was younger. He had a sly ease to him and a cocky grin that told a story of many mischievous actions he'd most likely been conducting his entire life. By the way that his mom and sister groaned at his remarks and playfully teased him, it was safe to say Jeremy was a character. But as a writer, I liked those types of people.

"What are you thinking about?" Mom smiled in my direction.

"What was that?"

"You seem a bit distracted this morning. How did things go over at your new friend's house?"

"It went well," I said.

"Yeah," she said expectantly. "Tell me about it."

"Well, they're a nice family," I started. "You'd like them. Bea is the girl I met, and she has a brother one year older than me. And their parents are quite nice, very in love, I think. Bea's dad is an English professor here at the local college."

"Really?" She sounded excited. "Did you tell him about your writing?"

"Yeah, a little."

"That could be a great connection for you, sweetie. We've heard nothing but good things about this school and—"

"Mom," I stopped her. "I'm going to Stanford. You know that's always been my plan."

"Well, plans can always change, honey. You might find more reasons to stay than go by that time."

"I know, but I've always dreamed of going there, like you and dad, and living somewhere by the beach."

"It's an amazing school, and your father and I had a great time there, but sometimes making your own path can lead you to treasures you may not have otherwise found."

I did not say anything. We stood in comfortable silence. The only sound was "Claire de Lune."

"I'd love help emptying some of these boxes. That is if you didn't have other plans," my mom said.

I would have to come up with a plan to see Bea again later. While I mindlessly emptied boxes filled with our treasured books, I remembered thinking that there was something tentative about the way Bea had talked about her future. I had the distinct feeling that Bea did not quite believe in herself or the face she showed to the world. It was strange. One minute she seemed confident and full of excitement for her future ideas and plans, and then something would come over her face, like a shadow, and I would catch a glimmer of sadness.

I checked my watch and decided it was finally late enough in the morning to head over. I broke down the now-empty boxes and smiled with satisfaction at the way I'd arranged our books in alphabetical order like Brandon's collection.

"Mom, I'm going to go for a run. I'll be back soon to help some more."

"Okay, Joel, say hello to Bea for me!" she called down from somewhere upstairs. I could never pull anything over on my mom. She was always two steps ahead of us all!

I set off, crossing the expansive lawn, ready to run at a slow pace, hoping to see a glimpse of a certain blonde neighbor. A few minutes later, I spotted Bea emerging from her front door, a bounce in her step as she walked down her driveway.

I watched her walking down the street, her golden hair tumbling past her shoulders, and I noted once again how beautiful she was. There was a natural grace about her, and she drew appreciative smiles from the neighbors as she passed, though she seemed lost in her own thoughts. I wondered what she was thinking about. Should I call out her name or just keep running? I did not want to scare her or seem like I was following her.

The distance between us was shortening, and the closer I got to her, the more nervous and dizzy I felt in her presence. I had just decided to call her name when she turned around and stopped us both in our tracks.

"Joel! Good morning! Are you following me?" she asked with a grin. Was she flirting with me?

"Good morning! Just thought I would go for a run and see more of the neighborhood," I said, feeling less confident than I was accustomed to feeling.

"Oh, . . . in your jeans?" she asked.

Something about this girl made me feel flustered. She had such a quick wit and a way of speaking that charmed me.

"You decided to take a safer mode of transportation today, I see." She pointed to my feet and smiled radiantly.

"Very funny! Yes. You got me. Actually, there's this crazy blonde neighbor I encountered yesterday who likes to hide in the bushes and scare innocent bystanders off their skateboards!"

We both laughed.

"Where are you headed?" I asked her, trying desperately to appear cool-headed and to distract her from remembering my embarrassing fall the day before.

"I'm on my way to spend time with a very special man."

"Oh," I said, my mind racing at the mention of a very special man.

"I work with a man named Peter. He used to be an attorney. He is eighty-six, and they won't let him out of the old age home until he is more mobile. It's sad. He was perfectly fine until he needed to get his gall bladder out a year ago. He wasn't being cared for properly, and his muscles atrophied within just days in the hospital bed."

I was impressed by this girl. She seemed to have many sides to her. "So, what do you do with him?"

"We do exercises. I try to get him up and moving every day so he can build some strength again."

"Wow, that's really great, Bea," I said. "Is this something you do on your own?"

"Yeah, Peter and I have a lot of one-on-one time, although his wife Tess comes by often to see him. You should see her. She is the same age, and she is always dressed in high fashion, her hair always impeccable. She even wears high heels, well, the old lady version. Still, she is a force to be reckoned with. Everyone clears the room when she walks in. Underneath, she's an absolute sweetheart, though. They are a very cute couple."

I smiled inwardly, seeing a side of Bea I had not expected. She was so comfortable and full of life when she spoke. Her apparent compassion was both refreshing and sweet. I was completely enamored by her.

"It probably seems strange to you, but there's really no one I'd enjoy spending time with more." She looked away and scanned the horizon while she walked, as if uncomfortable for having revealed a secret and was deep in thought. "But I should get going. Don't want to keep Peter waiting."

"Oh right, of course," I said, disappointed.

As if sensing my thoughts, she asked me, "What are you doing today?"

"Uhh . . . I'm not sure yet."

"Well," she said, shrugging, "would you like to come with me?"

My heart skipped a beat. "Oh, I don't want to be a third wheel," I joked.

"No, Peter would love it. He loves meeting new people. You will really like him. He tells some pretty wild stories."

Bea was looking at me, waiting for an answer. This was my chance to spend time with her. If she only knew that I would say yes, no matter what she was doing. What? You are on your way to visit a mass murderer? Sounds great! I noticed her watching me as she awaited my reply. Before I could say yes, she added, "Don't feel like you have to say yes. Not many people are looking to spend their day visiting with some old guy."

"Actually, I'd love to," I said.

She smiled and nodded. "Okay," she said, and we continued walking into town.

We walked up to Peter's temporary home. The grounds were lush with a beautifully maintained pond with benches situated under the shade all around it. There were several residents enjoying the morning sun. Once inside, it only took a quick glimpse at the luxurious décor to appreciate the quality of life that this home offered its residents. The beautiful grounds viewed through the glass windows at the back of the facility boasted countryside cottages on the one hundred and twenty scenic acres. Inside, beautiful crystal chandeliers lit up the main visiting room.

"Come on," Bea said as she half skipped toward the back deck. "Peter likes to sit and watch the pond. There are usually lots of ducks this time of year."

As far as I could tell, half the people here were half asleep and looked like they had given up, while the other half looked hopeful. Perhaps, like Peter, they hoped to return to family or to their homes.

Bea skipped over to a friendly looking man sitting in the shade. When he looked up and saw Bea, his face lit up. "There she is." He reached out toward her, and she gave him a hug.

Peter was a tall, slender man with a full head of white hair. He had eyes that were nearly as blue as Bea's and was very well-dressed. Peter glanced toward me, curious.

"Peter, I brought a friend today," Bea said, looking back at me.

I took a step forward to introduce myself. "Hello sir, my name is Joel Peterson." I extended my hand to him.

"Hello Joel, good to meet you," Peter said, taking my hand. His shake was gentle, his hands soft and worn.

"Same to you. Bea has told me a lot about you," I said.

"Don't believe anything she says," Peter joked.

"Oh, you know I think the world of you," Bea said, beaming at him. "Were you going to feed the ducks?"

"I think the ducks would quite enjoy that, yes," Peter said. Bea opened her backpack and pulled out half a loaf of bread.

I followed them to the pond as Bea helped Peter walk. He was very endearing. I had not spent much time around old people, never really knowing my grandparents. There was something sad but sweet about Peter. I knew his story for the most part after my walk here with Bea, but I now understood what she enjoyed about her time with him.

Bea gave Peter a piece of bread, and then me. The ducks noticed us right away and gathered near us. Bea threw a piece in, and a few ducks bobbed around in the water to snatch as much as they could. Then Peter broke his piece into many small pieces and threw them in at once. "Your turn Joel," Bea said.

I broke off a piece and noticed a small duck that the others were pushing away to get to the bread. He was not able to get a piece. I threw my entire piece of bread, so it landed in the water right in front of him. He quickly and excitedly snatched it up without the other ducks noticing. With a satisfied look, he nibbled happily.

We did this until the loaf was gone. The ducks were sure to be nice and fat this winter. Bea and I helped Peter back up to the building and went to his living quarters. Bea got Peter to play catch with a small red ball with a smiley face on it. I played too, and Peter seemed to enjoy it until he announced that he needed a nap. Bea helped him to bed and led me down to the lounge with large windows overlooking the pond.

We sat on the comfy chairs, and she pulled out two orange juices from her bag. "I always pack two," she said. I took one and popped it open to take a sip.

"I think Peter really liked you. You're really good with him," she said, trying to open her juice.

I extended my hand, and she reluctantly surrendered it to me so I could open it for her. "So, what did you think of him?" she asked.

"I think he's awesome," I said. "But I'm especially impressed with you. Not many girls would spend their time caring for some old guy, unrelated to her, simply because he needs help."

Bea smiled, embarrassed at my words. "It's no big deal. I have been doing this every day for months. I think I'd like to work with elderly people when I graduate."

"Would you like to go out with me sometime?" I said suddenly. At that moment, I was not nervous. I was sure that I had to get to know this girl, and I did not care if she knew that I was already crazy about her.

"Like . . . ," she said slowly, "for dinner?"

"Yes," I said, staring back at her.

A smile relaxed her face, and she looked like she wanted to laugh. "Sure," she said.

Sure had always been a plain and boring word to me. It was not even a yes; it was yes's less attractive younger sister. But, at that moment, *sure* sounded damn good to me.

CHAPTER THREE

I rushed home after leaving Bea at her driveway. I practically jumped through the door with excitement and ran up the stairs two at a time to my room. I unzipped my suitcase and began rummaging around for my dress shirts. I would have to iron one, of course, and I'd need to locate my Hugo Boss belt my mom had given me for my birthday one year.

I found what I needed, ironed a blue shirt, and hopped in the shower. The whole time I was in there, one thought went through my mind: I had a date with the most beautiful, kind, and smart girl I had ever met. When I was ready, I quickly jotted something in my journal.

September 14

I think I've waited for someone like Bea my whole life, and surely enough, after taking her sweet time, I'd met her. Only just yesterday morning, I was oblivious to the kind of excitement I felt tonight, our first date.

It was still too early to head over to her house, so I lay down on my bed and grabbed the book Brandon gave to me. *Treasure Island* was one of my favorite books from my childhood. It is a tale of buccaneers and buried gold, written by Robert Louis Stevenson. He was a Scottish novelist and travel writer, and much of his work had interested me even as a kid. At such a young age, I had decided this would be my life: to travel from one end of the beautiful world to the other. I could not wait to find out if Bea liked to travel and wondered about all the places she may have gone. This got me thinking about Peter and his wife. I bet they have had some incredible trips during their lifetimes. I made a mental note to ask him about it the next time I was with him.

Finally, the time came for me to leave and pick up Bea. Once again, my excitement had turned my nerves raw. I knew my parents and sister were out scoping out our new neighborhood and were thinking of grabbing a bite to eat at a local Italian restaurant they had heard good things about. I was glad there was no one home to witness my excitement. I had no idea how I would be able to hide my feelings for long and knew my mother had already suspected.

I walked down our stone walkway to the SUV since my family had taken my dad's new BMW. Before I got in the car, I went over to the lawn, where a bunch of wild daisies grew. I assumed my mom would have these taken away soon, as they were weeds. But something about them reminded me of Bea. They were unassumingly beautiful, like her, and sweet too. I plucked one from the grass and put it in my shirt pocket. I got into the car, and with one last check in the mirror and a big breath, I was on my way.

As I drove up the Canning's driveway, I immediately saw Bea, sitting on the porch swing. She looked up and offered me the kind of smile that never ceased to move me. Bea, as beautiful as ever, stood up and walked toward me. She had her hair set loosely around her shoulders, and she wore a cream-colored sundress with the faintest pattern of flowers.

I cut the engine and got out of the car, walking up to the steps as she met me there.

"Hey," she said, smiling.

"Hey," I said. "You look beautiful."

She blushed a little, giving me some encouragement. "Thank you."

I pulled out the small daisy I had put in my shirt pocket on the way down the driveway and extended it to her.

She laughed and took the little flower. "What a gentleman," she teased, but she looked quite touched. She put it in her hair behind her ear.

I thought it completed her look perfectly, with an effortless ease I had never known any other girl to have. I did not like a lot of makeup and fake nails. Bea was very natural and soft. She did not wear a lot of makeup, and her hair was always just a little tousled.

On the way to dinner, we talked about what we had done since we parted ways earlier, and then before we knew it, Siri announced that we had arrived at our destination.

"Where are you taking me?" Bea asked, curiosity drenching each word.

"I hope you're hungry!" I replied, giving her a wink.

"I should probably be taking you somewhere, Mr. California," Bea said as we turned into the parking lot.

I had already done my research on the local eats before moving. San Diego is known for its great restaurants and diversity in cuisines, so I, of course, made sure I would have my staples like Mexican, Italian, and Japanese. I was taking Bea to a Teppanyaki restaurant, a style of Japanese cuisine that uses an iron griddle to cook food in front of you, with a show included. There is one in Saratoga called Duo. Located on 175 South Broadway in the heart of Saratoga Springs, the elegant restaurant provided guests with a truly unique dining experience.

"Wow, I've actually never been here," Bea said, sounding impressed. "Alright, Joel, I'm very curious about you."

"Why's that?" I asked as I looked for a good parking spot.

"In your first two days in Saratoga Springs, you have had a near-death experience, met my entire family, won over Peter, and taken me to maybe the one restaurant in my hometown I've never been to."

"Well, sometimes things are just meant to happen a certain way," I said, smiling.

"Maybe," Bea said quietly to herself.

Inside the restaurant, it was beautifully decorated. Japanese paper umbrellas lined the entryway. Within the double doors, we found black candlelit tables occupied by well-dressed couples of all ages and even a few families. At the entrance, a glass staircase led up to where I knew we would be seated.

"Hello, welcome to Duo," said a girl in a kimono situated at the host's podium. "Do you have a reservation?"

"Yes, it's under Peterson," I said to her. I stole a glance at Bea, who was looking intently at our surroundings.

"Right this way," the girl said. She led us up the staircase and to the last griddle on the upper level.

There were a dozen seats surrounding it, with candles and small glass orbs with lilies inside. We were the first to be seated along one edge. The chef wore a tall white chef's hat and was busy sharpening his knives, readying himself for his live show. The idea of Teppanyaki is to bring entertainment to the table. He had a confident air about him as he glanced around the room, taking it all in. Bea's eyes were darting all around the room as well.

"Are you excited?" I asked her with a smile.

"Are you kidding? I have not been to one of these since I was a kid. What a fantastic idea, Joel." Her sweet smile was enough to satisfy me for days. I cannot imagine what effect watching her enjoying the show will have on me. I was starved and would normally have preferred an intimate table for two until I freaked out about whether we would have anything to talk about. I was so in over my head. I said a silent prayer that everything would go amazingly.

The seats around us slowly filled with a friendly couple who sat next to us, and a family of six filled out the rest of the table. We all introduced ourselves quickly, and the others continued talking amongst themselves. Bea and I sat there smiling at each other, both obviously a little nervous. She still had the flower in her hair.

Then our chef came back with a rolling table filled with food. "Hello, and good evening everyone!" he said loudly. "I am chef Kato. I will be preparing your meal tonight. Anyone have any food allergies?"

A few people said no, and the rest of us shook our heads. "Wonderful," he shouted. And then out of nowhere, he pulled out two knives and started doing tricks. Everyone cheered, including Bea. I could not stop stealing glances in her direction. He poured oil and white rice onto the griddle and then pulled out a few eggs. He cracked the eggs with the knives while they spun on the cooktop, and everyone cheered again.

He started cooking an assortment of veggies along with small pieces of chicken, beef, and salmon. It all smelled delicious. A waiter came around with small appetizers of salmon teriyaki maki rolls and wakame salad as we waited for the main entrée to finish cooking.

Bea took a bite of her roll, and I waited to see her reaction before digging into mine. As she chewed, a smile grew on her face, and her eyes sparkled happily.

I laughed. "Is it good?"

"Mmmmm," she said with her mouth full and gave me a thumbs up.

I tried mine, and it was absolute heaven. I poured her more tea, and she thanked me as she took a sip.

"This is delicious," she said to me.

"I'm glad," I said. "Something tells me you enjoy food." I nudged her playfully.

She laughed. "I do. Sometimes more than people. But Japanese is my favorite."

I beamed at her. I had picked her favorite without even knowing!

Chef Kato went on with the show, even taking pieces of broccoli and tossing them into his audience's mouths with his knife. Bea was the only one who caught hers, to my surprise and everyone's delight. They clapped and cheered for her, and she grinned while she chewed.

Dinner was a huge success and delicious too. We ended up not needing to talk too much, aside from small talk in between tricks or asking if the other wanted more tea. I wasn't upset about this since just being with Bea was comfortable and nice.

We left the restaurant as it was getting dark. "Want to go for a walk?" Bea asked, looking up at the night sky. It was still warm enough to go without a sweater, and the fireflies were out.

"Sure," I said. We started walking down the street as families played Frisbee and catch in the park across the way.

"When I was a kid, Jeremy and I would try to catch fireflies and put them in jars," Bea said. "Do you have siblings?"

I could not believe my sister had not come up yet. I had told her very little about myself, I realized. I was so curious about her that I forgot. "Yeah, I have a twin sister, actually," I said.

"Really? You're a twin?" she said, a little surprised.

"Yeah, her name is Anna, and she's pretty cool. She looks like the girl version of me pretty much."

"Well, that's unfortunate for her," Bea said, knocking her arm into mine.

"Hey now, who just took you for a meal that you said, and I quote, 'was the best Japanese you'd ever had.'"

"Some guy who can't ride a skateboard to save his life." She grinned.

"Alright, that's fair," I said in defeat.

"Who's older, you or Anna?"

"I am, by six minutes."

Bea nodded and looked down at her shoes. "Well, I'd love to meet your family sometime."

"Yeah, they'd like you," I said with encouragement. "My parents are really cool too. You can come for dinner sometime."

"Okay," she said.

"Okay," I echoed. "Bea?"

"Yes?"

We were stopped now on the path in the park, the fireflies sparkling around us, the heat and last of the twilight enveloping us into our own bubble of a perfect night.

"Do you have any fears?" I asked, attempting to start a philosophical conversation.

"Only a few," Bea said hesitantly. Then she started walking again.

I felt like I hit a sore spot for her. I had not expected my question to make her uncomfortable, so I certainly didn't stay on it.

"So, what are some other things you and Jeremy did as kids?" I asked.

"Our childhood mostly consisted of Jer getting us in trouble and me getting us out," she answered with a laugh. I relaxed a bit at the sound of her laugh, feeling like I had not blown it yet.

"Ah, see, Anna and I were both trouble-makers. So, we would almost always get caught. Didn't stop us from trying, though!"

"Hmm, so do you think you've outgrown it?"

"Definitely not," I said, grinning. "Causing trouble since we could walk, can't give up on it now."

Bea smiled at me and looked like she was about to say something else but decided not to.

We were in the center of the park, where an old fountain stood. The water fell from a basin on top of a woman's head and trickled down around her. It was such a beautiful night, and with the fireflies, the sound of the fountain, and a busker playing "Dream a Little Dream of Me" on a harmonica, I could not imagine a more perfect backdrop. I really did not miss San Diego yet. My new world had filled me with hope and small-town charm. My new friends I had found in the Canning family had me excited, and every time I thought of Bea, I felt happy in a way like I could not imagine ever being sad again.

Bea sat down on the edge of the fountain and closed her eyes with a smile on her pretty face. "What a perfect night," she said. It was hard not to notice. I had somehow gotten it right today, and to my delight, this perfect girl had a great time with me. I already could not wait to see her again.

September 14

The stars were brighter tonight, the air warmer, sweeter. The fall flowers were in their last weeks of bloom before the inevitable east coast cold. I was not worried about my first fall. I had come across a smile so warm that I would keep summer with me all winter. My dinner with Bea was perfect. She is perfect. If only I could peek inside her mind to know if she felt the same way about me.

CHAPTER FOUR

⬤⟨◇⟩⬤

M y new school was better than I thought, as was the change of seasons. There was a bite in the air, something I had little experience with. Last weekend we took a family trip to the city to go shopping for fall clothes, which was my mother's idea. It was fun. Anna, my mom, and I had never been to New York City, and we all thought it was cool.

The leaves were turning to gold and orange, and there were street vendors selling pretzels and roasted chestnuts. We had gone to the Met Museum to check out some of the exhibits, and we went nuts in the gift shop. There was the most incredible assortment of books, all about art and history. I was in heaven, and we must have spent an hour in there, at least. I left with a couple of pins and some books about some of the artists we saw in the museum. Then we walked around Central Park, got hot dogs, and sat in the grass by the pond. That trip had been my favorite memory since arriving in New York State, apart from my first dinner with Bea.

It had been almost a month since that dinner, and I was spending more and more time with Bea. She was incredibly smart, and I learned she shared my passion for travel. In her room, she had a big world map, with pins on all the places she wanted to go and sticky notes with information on things she wants to see in each place.

I was also spending more time with Jeremy. We would go skateboarding or play soccer in his backyard. I had visited him a couple of times at his campus, where he had shown me around and introduced me to girls. He was completely unaware of my feelings toward his sister, which I thought was best for now.

I still had not figured out how Bea felt about me entirely. Neither of us was flirty by nature, but we were very compatible on an intellectual level, something I had never experienced with a girl my age. I could have real conversations with her about things that mattered, and she had intelligent opinions and knowledge on any subject I brought up. Bea had an opinion for everything, usually a strong one if morals were involved. She was a good person and cared deeply for the creatures in this world, whether they were four-legged, two-legged, winged, or finned.

Her kindness was something I loved about her. I loved how she cared for an elderly man she was not related to, simply because she enjoyed it, or how she volunteered at the animal shelter on Mondays. She would also go to the children's hospital in the city once a month to read to the kids and spend time with them. Jeremy had told me their family was a big supporter of the children's hospital and donated money every year, which I thought was cool to do. I thought they did it simply because they could afford it, which was amazing.

When we were walking through Times Square last weekend, we had passed by people standing in line to get into one of the many Broadway shows. I looked up and saw *The Phantom of the*

Opera headlining at one of the old theatres. I remembered seeing a poster for this musical in Bea's room and decided I would take her to see it. I ordered two tickets in the most amazing seats for the following Saturday, which was now tomorrow.

I had bought two Phantom masks while I had been in the city, and later in the week, I put one on and knocked on Bea's door. When she answered, a smile slowly grew on her pretty face. I handed her the other mask and told her we were going to see it in a few days. She was very excited and put her mask on in the doorway. She invited me in, and we listened to the soundtrack while Jeremy crinkled his nose and made funny comments. Bea did not seem to mind. She listened to the music with a faraway look in her eyes, maybe imagining being at the theatre and hearing it live. Another point for me!

I sat propped up in bed at 10:30 p.m. on Friday, checking that the tickets were all good and making sure my clothes for the following day were wrinkle-free. I could not wait. This would be our second official date if Bea even considered them dates. She was sweet and kind, but I was always wondering what she really thought about me. Did she like me the way I liked her? Did she think about me as often as I thought about having her ocean blue eyes looking up at me again? I think for the first couple weeks of knowing each other, she seemed a little uncertain about me, possibly because I was always finding an excuse to see her. I'd go over with the façade of borrowing a book, hanging out with Jeremy, or even showing her dad something I'd written. I grabbed my journal and popped the cap off my favorite Japanese felt pen.

Tomorrow I will try to get my answer, try to find out what she is thinking. She's become the single occupant within my mind. Her laugh has become my drug of choice. I'm going to make a move tomorrow, and one way or another, I will finally know. She might crush my heart, I might suffer a huge disappointment, or I might come home filled with light. Either way, I'll have my answer.

The alarm went off at 7:00 a.m., and I shot out of bed. I was picking up Bea in half an hour to drive to the train station. We were attending the matinee, so we would not get home too late. The show started at 1 p.m., and it was a good two-hour train ride into the city. I was wearing a pair of grey pants with a pale blue dress shirt, my Steve Madden brown dress shoes, and the charcoal pea-coat that I got the weekend prior. I put it all on and looked in the mirror. I looked good. My hair was washed the night before, and I quickly ran a comb through it, brushed my teeth, and I was out the door.

When I got to Bea's, I sent her a text instead of going to the door so that I did not wake anyone up.

Joel: *Hey! I'm here!*

She responded almost right away.

Bea: *K coming :)*

A moment later, she appeared. She wore a burgundy coat that reached her knees and tied at the waist, and she had black nylons on with low black heels. I knew Bea was way too smart to wear uncomfortable shoes on our adventure, so I assumed these heels were comfy. She carried the small black leather bag by a brand she had said was called Fossil. It went over her shoulder and across her torso, and she would wear it instead of carrying a purse. She had explained how much she hated carrying things in the early stages of knowing her. She did not even like to walk with a drink in her hand. I discovered this once when we went to grab a coffee, and I had made the mistake of suggesting a walk along the main street. I got the lowdown that day on this strange but charming quirk.

I was in the SUV and smiled as Bea got into the passenger's seat. "Good morning."

"Morning!" Bea said cheerfully. "I'm so excited!" She cupped her face in her hands, and her eyes sparkled.

"Me too!" I said, very pleased. "I hope it's as good as you're hoping. I think I got some great seats!" I started the car and turned around in her driveway.

"I've heard really good things about this production," Bea said. "I was up late reading reviews last night."

"Oh yeah?" I asked as I pulled out onto our street. "That's awesome. I've never actually seen a musical before."

"Really? So, what made you want to see this one?" she asked curiously.

"Uhhhh . . . ," I hesitated. "Well, you, actually."

"I see," she said. I peeked at her and saw she was smiling.

Bea navigated us to the train station, and we listened to my favorite indie band from L.A., The Local Natives. I had played them for Bea last week, and she had loved them. When we reached the train station, we parked, bought our tickets, and bought two blueberry muffins from the concession stand.

We sat and ate them on a bench on the platform, while other early birds waited with us for the next train. Some were dressed in suits, and others had big backpacks and good walking shoes. You could tell who was a commuter and who was a tourist.

It felt cool to think I lived here. There were things I missed about California, like the beach and the familiar Spanish tile rooftops and stucco, but I was really enjoying the crisp weather and the beautiful fall colors. The buildings here were much older than in San Diego and expressed a lot of history from this area. There were monuments and heritage buildings, some from the war of 1812, others from the 1900s. Everything was more colorful and vibrant, with a story around every corner.

Bea ate her muffin quickly and followed it with an orange juice she had brought from home. Of course, she brought two like she said she always did and handed one to me.

"Thanks, Miss Ready-for-Anything," I said.

Bea laughed. "I will admit I like to come prepared. Hey, will we have time for a quick stop before the show? There's somewhere I want to take you."

"Yeah, sure," I said. "The show doesn't start until one, and we should get to Grand Central by about eleven-thirty."

"Perfect! Since you surprised me with these tickets, this will be my treat. Every true New Yorker has to try this as a rite of passage."

"Wow, well, I'm very intrigued. Can I know what I'm trying?"

"It's a surprise, but trust me, you'll love it."

The train ride flew by as Bea and I had a lot to talk about as usual. We listened to music, taking turns listening to the songs we loved, and she showed me different landmarks as we looked out the window.

We arrived at Grand Central Terminal just before noon, and Bea seemed to know where she was going. The city was very busy, with people of every sort out and about enjoying their Saturday. We passed buskers, street vendors, and crazy people shouting about the end of the world as we made our way to find a taxi. We went straight to Times Square and made it there in ten minutes. Bea continued leading me through the crowds and past the many sights and smells. We made it to a restaurant that had a sign on the window that read, "The Best Cheesecake on the Planet!" The restaurant was called Junior's Restaurant and Bakery. Bea grinned. "We're here!" she announced.

We ducked inside, and I was surprised by what I saw. I had never seen a restaurant so sprawling and busy. We were seated right away, and as the hostess led us to a table, she looked back several times to make sure we were still in tow. It looked very regular, and the food in front of many of the diners was served in red plastic baskets containing pickles, thick-cut French fries, and massive burgers. I bet Jeremy loves it here, I thought with a little chuckle. I had never seen anyone eat so much in my life. Jeremy would literally inhale any food put in front of him. It was both amazing and slightly worrisome.

We were seated at a table for two in the center of the busy restaurant, and Bea and I took off our jackets and got comfortable. The hostess gave us two plastic menus and left us to decide what we were having.

"So, you can get whatever you want, but you have to get cheese-cake," Bea said excitedly.

"Oh, I have to, huh?" I said, teasing.

"Yes, you actually do! You can't come to New York without try-ing Junior's cheesecake. It's the best there is. I recommend the raspberry, my favorite."

I did not have to look at the menu. The excitement in Bea's eyes told me her choice must be something good. I noticed she had very good taste and truly appreciated the best. Her love of food, well, it was just so cute. For such a tiny girl, she sure talked a lot about food. As a matter of fact, she was always eating too. She always had food in her myriad bags, no matter where she seemed to go.

A thin waiter with glasses and an awkward teenage shuffle showed up. "What'll you have today?"

I stole a glance at Bea, who was smiling as though she was keep-ing the biggest secret. "We'll have two pieces of the raspberry cheesecake, please, and a glass of water, no ice, please."

"I'll have water too, please!" Bea said politely.

"Coming up."

"So, I can hardly wait to try it. How many times have you been here?" I asked Bea, noticing how some of her hair was springing into tiny soft curls in the warm restaurant.

"I've only been a few times with my family. We don't travel far from home. My family are a bunch of homebodies. Everyone but me that is. I've always wanted to go someplace new, see what's out there, you know?" Her voice trailed off.

Our cheesecake was to die for amazing. I did not think anything could taste as good. Bea wore a satisfied look on her face as we made our way toward the theater.

My excitement was growing with each step as we approached the massive structure. I wondered about all the millions of people who had come before us to watch the very same show. *The Phantom of the Opera* was in a league of its own. It was known for its love story and hauntingly beautiful music. I was more excited to be spending time with Bea, and the fact that we would be seated side by side for the next three hours made me extremely happy but also very nervous. It was my first time seeing a big production, and although I'd always wanted to see one, to see my first with someone I was head over heels for, well, let's just say my heart was racing like a rocket speeding to the moon.

I looked around at the people slowly making their way inside the theatre, and I smiled inwardly, knowing they were all there for the same reason we were. As the usher walked us toward our seats in the middle of the first row of the first balcony, everyone else faded into the background. When the lights lowered and the music began, I felt like we were the only ones there, and the play had been put together just for us.

My heart began to race, and my hands were sweaty as I wondered how I would possibly be able to stand being so close to Bea without melting. But when the play started, I became captivated with the scenes unfolding in front of us, and my senses became fixated on the feeling of the music as its beauty coursed through my veins.

I felt Bea's knee rest beside mine, and my body became electrified. I stole a few glances her way and watched as her face contorted with emotion as Bea became absorbed in the music. She closed her eyes, and when she reopened them, they were glistening with tears. It was amazing to experience so many intense longings and emotions. I was not expecting any of this.

Our knees felt like they were fused in an erotic pose, and neither of us dared to move for fear of severing the exhilarating vibration. With our bodies touching the whole time, I did not want anything else in the world and would have been happy to sit there, next to Bea, for eternity.

Intermission came, and we stayed locked together, side by side. We were completely happy to remain seated, quiet, each of us lost in our own thoughts. There were no words to describe the intense feeling between us. I looked around in awe of the majestic surroundings, the gilded walls, the oversized chandeliers, and heavy red and gold drapes that separated the magical scenes from the observers.

Once the play ended, we rose quietly and followed the crowd into the lobby and out the doors into the bright afternoon sunshine.

"Wow! That was incredible. The phantom's voice was amazing, wasn't it?" I asked her. "What did you think, Bea?"

"I absolutely loved it. I mean, think about the story—an obsession of a disfigured and murderous musical genius who lives beneath the Paris Opera House and the fate of never being seen for the person you are inside. His love for her broke my heart completely. I'm never going to get over it!"

I laughed softly.

"What?! How can you laugh at me?" Bea shoved me as she began giggling. Soon, we were both laughing like crazy, and each time one of us showed signs of slowing down, we would both laugh even harder.

"Oh man, you're amazing, Bea!"

We began walking toward the trains. It seemed as though something had changed between us. We were closer, and there seemed to be a seriousness between us. I felt my breathing intensify, and the electricity remained strong. My body was on fire, and all I wanted to do was grab her and kiss her. I wondered if she felt it too. I stared at her lips and at the curve of her neck while she scanned the ads along the inside of the train, the echo of the tracks competing with the beating of my racing heart.

Once we were seated on the train, I reached for Bea's hand, which was curled into a gentle fist on her lap. I covered her hand with mine, and she looked into my eyes. I could not look away, afraid to interrupt the exchange and the sweetness of the moment. I remained still, my hand covering hers.

After a few minutes, Bea turned her hand into mine, and as our fingers laced together, my desire for this person grew. I never would have thought in a million years that holding hands with a girl could cause such a swell of feeling and emotion inside of me. *That was just it*, I thought to myself. *This was not just a girl. This was the girl.*

I had heard of love at first sight, read books about it, watched movies about it, and nurtured the hope that it might be true. But when I experienced it firsthand, I felt both lost and found—lost because I knew I needed her, like I needed oxygen, and found because I seemed to have found myself when I was with her.

I have always liked to spend time alone, enjoyed my own company, and felt good about the guy I was. It seemed people liked me, and girls had always smiled at me encouragingly—guys too, to my chagrin. But when I was with Bea, I felt like I was funnier, smarter, more interesting, and more interested in life. The world, everything, and everyone became sublimely important. I wanted to see, feel, smell, taste, touch everything, everyone, everywhere all at once.

I began to visualize Bea and myself together, holding hands, smiling, laughing, discovering all that life had to offer. I had read in a book once, all you needed to do was to see it and believe it, and everything you wanted would become yours. So, I decided to think intentionally about my heart's desire—to spend my days and nights with Bea.

We stepped off the train and walked toward my car. It was so amazing. We walked in comfortable silence, each enjoying the moment, our own thoughts and feelings, and the world unfolding around us. It was such a relief that we didn't feel the need to stuff conversation into the minutes that ticked by. It was enough for us to ride the wave of the comfortable vibration that joined us.

Once back in Bea's driveway, we got out of the car and walked toward Bea's front door. I began to smile. Bea looked over at me, saw the smile, and smiled too.

"Later!" I said, and she laughed out loud.

"Later!" she returned and walked into the house, offering up a small wave as the hem of her dress floated in behind her as the door closed.

CHAPTER FIVE

I awoke to the sound of Chopin, one of my sister's favorite composers. Anna learned how to play the piano when she was four years old. There had been a retired concert pianist who lived down the road from us back home, and he gave lessons. His name was Marc, and he was from Canada. He lived with his wife and two kids who were two years older than Anna and me, and they were twins too! Our moms met at a kindergarten function, and Anna had been blown away by the kids' ability to play the piano as they performed a duet for the class.

My mom would walk her down every Saturday morning at 9:00 a.m. no matter what. Anna was the first person in our family to show any talent musically, and she quickly became known in our school and community as the protégé. Growing up, our parents always had different genres of music playing in the background, anything from Johnny Cash, Michael Bublé, and Josh Grobin to opera and classical. They even played modern country and western. It was amazing.

I went downstairs in my pajamas, sent a quick text to Bea, and once I got into the kitchen, I realized I was smiling from ear to ear.

Joel: *Morning beautiful. Can't wait to look into those beautiful blue eyes again.*

Bea: *Good morning! I can't wait to see you too.*

I could not shake the image of Bea from my mind. The intense feelings between us the previous day had my heart still racing. It was a miracle that I even slept. I grabbed a mug and helped myself to a cup of hot steaming coffee, with the melody of Anna's music reminding me of the incredible performance I saw just last night.

"Hey, Sis, do you know any songs from *Phantom of the Opera*?" I asked, coming into the great room where our grand piano had been delivered and set up.

"I actually know two," she said, looking up from the keys. "How was last night?"

"It was great, and the production was amazing," I said.

"You know I meant something else," Anna replied with a grin.

I just laughed and shook my head. "Do you know 'Think of Me'?"

Instead of answering me, Anna turned back to the gleaming white keys and started playing. I was immediately transported back to the theatre. I could still feel Bea's knee next to mine.

"Well," Anna said, stopping the music. I realized she was looking at me. "It's about time you fell in love."

"I don't know what you're talking about," I said, shrugging.

"Yes, you do," Anna said. "And I don't blame you. She is kind of perfect. Too bad you will probably screw it up. It's definitely all downhill from here."

"I never knew I had such a funny sister," I said, crossing my arms.

"You'll probably scare her away with your intense longing gazes."

"Or I'll end up marrying this girl," I said, not knowing where my words came from.

My mother, with her impeccable timing, chose that precise moment to waltz in through the sliding glass door of the back patio where she had been refilling the bird feeders. Her face registered shock when she asked, "Did I just hear correctly? Someone is getting married?"

I was feeling on top of the world, so why not admit it. "Yep! Bea and I are going to get married one day."

"Who's getting married?" my dad asked, coming into the room in a pair of jogging pants and a hoodie. He looked sweaty and had his headphones around his neck, seemingly just back from a jog.

"Joel and Bea! C'mon Dad, get with the program!" Anna joked, walking toward the staircase to head up to her room.

My dad just smiled and assured me that Bea was a great catch. I knew they thought I was just kidding around. Little did they know I was dead serious. I knew we were young, but when you know, you know. I walked out the front door and headed to Bea's while I texted her.

Joel: *Good morning! I wanted to give you a head's up that your dad and I are going over one of my papers in 10.*

I was super excited to hear his constructive criticism on my paper on *Don Quixote*, the Spanish novel by Miguel de Cervantes. The plot revolves around the adventures of a noble from La Mancha named Alonso Quixano, who reads so many chivalric romances that he loses his mind! Imagine, ladies and gentlemen, a book about chivalry and romance. I laughed at myself for being such a romantic fool.

I continued to walk toward the Canning's house when my phone pinged. *See you soon!* Bea texted back. I smiled and walked a little quicker.

After I chatted with Bea and her mom over a second cup of coffee, Brandon opened the beautifully carved wooden door to his office and waved me in, one hand holding his phone to his ear, his crisp blue polo shirt tucked neatly into his Ralph Lauren slacks. I noticed he was wearing a pair of Girotti handmade Italian shoes made from luxurious leather and stamped with the owner's name on the bottom. I remembered learning about them when we went shopping a few weeks ago. My mom and sister were drooling over the display in the West Village.

The man had taste, I thought to myself, as I followed him nervously into his office. The room was floor to ceiling cherry wood. The walls were covered with built-in bookcases with richly colored books in an array of sizes. Brandon's desk was a beautiful design with rich, ornate details that looked like they would stand the test of time. Hand-carved architectural details on the dark wood finishing with warm hues made it a classic piece of art rather than a piece of furniture.

Ruched satin curtain panels spanned two to three times the width of the large bay window opening and hung from the ceiling to the floor. Their color resembled platinum and matched the crystal table lamps, which lit up every corner of the office. I detected the faint aroma of books, a smell that I could only describe as equal parts woody, smoky, earthy, and vanilla. The intensity of the smell grew as I passed the books which were located closest to the large window with the autumn sunshine pouring through.

I had been in Brandon's office for about twenty minutes when Bea burst in, her ponytail flailing behind her as she ran over, out of breath and tears lighting up her eyes.

"Dad, Peter had a bad fall and is in the hospital. Tess just called me. I have to hurry!" She turned around and began to run back out of Brandon's office, shouting over her shoulder that she would meet us there.

Mr. Canning and I arrived at the emergency room entrance moments later and found Bea and her mom standing off in the corner closest to the front nurses' station.

"Don't worry, dear, he'll be okay," said a nearby nurse, offering Bea a small hug. I thought that seemed odd, but it seemed as though she knew Bea and her mom. As we approached, Bea noticed us and rushed over, relief washing over her face.

"How is he?" Brandon asked her.

It turned out that Peter and his wife Tess were very much loved by the entire Canning family. He was a special guy, I had to admit. His wife had also found a special place in Bea's heart, and I marveled at the outward affection they all shared. It was as though they shared more than a relationship. There seemed to be a deep connection between Bea and Peter, as though time and age could never keep them hostage from experiencing the deepest of connections.

Bea continued speaking to the nurses at the nurses' station. They all seemed to know her by name. My mind began racing, trying to piece together how everyone fit together and knew each other. I took a step closer and hoped Bea would notice I was there. One of the nurses with dark hair in a bun looked over her shoulder at me. Seeing the nurse's attention settle on something beyond her, Bea turned suddenly and gave me a hopeful look while she extended her hand toward me. I reached out and took her hand quickly, hoping she would not have the chance to retract it.

"This is my friend Joel," she introduced me to the nurses, all looking pleased. Once again, I got the distinct feeling that I was on the other side of some sort of secret or confidence. I was intent on figuring this out later when I had time to myself to think.

Two other nearby nurses smiled warmly in my direction, having noticed Bea holding my hand.

"How's he doing?" I asked Bea, trying not to show my distraction.

My hand, which she was still holding, began to tingle. This was the same hand I had held on the train, I thought. I felt goosebumps form on the back of my neck.

"He's got a broken hip and two fractured ribs. They said he's pretty bruised up too." Her voice betrayed her concern as she hung her head and cried quietly. I did not know what to say. I hated hospitals. I tried to avoid them at all costs.

"Do you know what happened?" I asked.

All I was able to learn was that Peter and Tess had a meeting with his doctor, who was determined to turn his temporary home into a more permanent setting. When Peter asked what he had to do to prove to them he would be fine once he was allowed to return home, his doctor told him he would have to be able to walk unassisted up and down the hall several times. So, Peter had been practicing walking at night when the retirement home was quiet. They found him sprawled on the floor with a gash on his head and bruises all over. He had made it to the front door but could not manage to get the heavy door open. They believe he hit himself in the head and got knocked out, breaking his hip and ribs on the way down.

"I'm sorry, Bea. If there's anything I can do . . . ."

"Thank you for coming, Joel. I'm going to find out when I can go in and see him."

"I'll wait for you with your parents," I said. "I'm not going anywhere."

Bea smiled up at me, relief flashing over her face before the tension reappeared in her brow.

Looking around as I waited, I noticed it was a very nice hospital. As I approached the cafeteria, I watched a team of surgeons walk by, lost in their trade talk. Before turning the corner, I looked back to see whether Bea had returned, and I saw that the surgeons seemed to recognize Mr. and Mrs. Canning. They acknowledged them with nods or smiles, while one stopped to talk, a sympathetic expression upon his face.

I stopped in my tracks and watched, and from where I stood, I faintly heard Bea's name. Brandon and Ria looked equally strained and grief-stricken. I wondered about the possibility of their family being big supporters of the hospital or something. It would not surprise me. But there was something else going on. The nurses and doctors all shared a similar expression while speaking to Bea and her family. It seemed to be sympathy mixed with sadness.

I ordered three coffees from the cafeteria and brought them back to Mr. and Mrs. Canning. Fifteen minutes later, Bea emerged and announced that Peter was doing amazingly well. She said she did not want to go home until his wife, Tess, arrived. "You should have seen him. He was even cracking his jokes and trying to make me laugh."

Bea's mom and dad asked if they could drop me back off at home, as Bea would likely be a while. I gave Bea a hug before we left, and as we started walking, Bea's mom turned around and warned Bea not to overdo it. Bea looked embarrassed and upset, which was a new and strange reaction for me to witness. She did not reply to this. She just looked at me and gave me a quick smile before going back to Peter's room.

The next day I picked Bea up, and we went to see Peter together. We stopped to get him some flowers from Bea's favorite shop in town. I offered to pay, and we picked out some big, vibrant sunflowers. Bea said Peter loved them, and they were the second-best thing after the actual sun.

When we got to the hospital, many nurses and doctors said hello to Bea again. I was beginning to wonder what that was all about but knew it would be rude to ask. I thought maybe she had broken something and had spent some time here before, or it simply could be that it was such a small town that most people knew each other here. I knew I saw the same faces at the local coffee shop and at the grocery store.

Bea opened the door to Peter's room and peeked in. "Peter?"

"Hello, love," I heard Peter's gentle voice say back.

She opened the door, and we went inside. Peter was pretty bruised up, and he had some gauze over the gash on his forehead. It was hard to see such a kind man looking so beat up. My heart ached for him, not being able to spend the last part of his life enjoying his beautiful home and the company of his loving wife.

"Hi Peter, I brought Joel today," Bea said sweetly.

"Hey Peter, how are you feeling?" I asked as I reached his bed.

"Just splendid, my friend," Peter said with a twinkle in his eye. "I'll be out of here in no time, I'm sure. Good thing I have my personal trainer to whip me into shape." He winked at Bea.

Bea took his hand in hers. "Yes, we're going to get you back home," she said. "You'll be sitting in your garden with Tess this spring, just in time for the cherry blossoms."

"I do love Sakura season," Peter said.

"Hopefully, you love sunflowers too," I said, opening the tissue so he could see the flowers in my arms. "We got you these to brighten up the room."

"Oh, how nice, thank you," Peter said, looking pleased. "I'll have Tess bring our big vase later today."

I set them down on the nearby counter and took off my jacket. Bea sat on the edge of Peter's bed while I took a seat on the chair in the corner of the room.

"You two would make a lovely couple, you know," Peter said, smiling at both of us. I could see Bea's cheeks turn flaming red, as she did not dare to look at me. My heart jumped in my chest at this elderly man's sweet remark.

"I have always hoped you'd find someone worthy of your beauty, my dear," Peter said. "It would seem as though now you have . . . ," Peter's voice trailed off as his eyes closed, and his breathing deepened in sleep.

Bea was quiet, and I did not dare to say anything about Peter's musings, but I felt elated to know this was what he thought of me. I only hoped Bea had started feeling the same way.

"I'm going to go get us some tea," I said. I got up and left the room, the girl I loved watching me as I did.

Later that night, alone in my room, with my journal propped up on my knees in bed, I thought about the brief conversation my sister and I had earlier. *Marriage*. Funny how you get to an age, and suddenly life becomes real. Thinking about Bea, I knew I was the marrying type. To me, being part of a couple that includes her feels right. The idea of spending time with one woman who adored me as much as I adored her struck me as, well, the best thing that life could offer.

I wanted it all—love, marriage, kids. I knew it had only been a few months since I had met Bea, but it felt like I'd always known her somehow. I thought of Peter and how his voice grew gentle when he spoke of his wife of forty years. I wanted to grow old together with someone I trusted and could share the joy and wonders of this amazing world. I wanted to travel with her and see and experience new places and discover a myriad of wonders around the world.

CHAPTER SIX

December 20

Bea is going to be so shocked when she sees her Christmas present. Jeremy will laugh when he sees his. Can't wait to see them tonight. It's crazy how much things have changed, how important these people have become to me!

I was settling in nicely here in Saratoga Springs, my life feeling much fuller than it ever had. I had amazing new friends, and our families got along great. When I was not with Bea, I was often hanging out with Jeremy. Or, our families would get together for dinner, taking turns as hosts. I was doing well in school and practicing college essays with Bea's father. I felt so happy these last few months. I even discovered that I liked snow!

As fall came and went, we shared many meals and laughs. Bea and I had been hiking. We would swap books, stay up all night on her porch, and talk on the weekends. Bea, Jeremy, Anna, and I had even taken a trip to New York City one weekend, eating at Wahlburgers and street meat vendors, and walking around Central Park. Bea and I went off and visited the famous library on

Fifth Avenue, both of us enamored with the beauty and massive collection of incredible literature and history. We all got along great. Bea and Anna had even become friends.

It was 8:00 p.m. on our first day of Christmas break, and I was about to leave with Anna to go to Bea and Jeremy's. We were exchanging presents tonight, and I could not wait to give Bea her gift. We were going snow tubing later tonight—my and Anna's first time. Bea said I would love it. I skimmed through my journal, remembering all the warm memories with each written word. Then I got off my bed and walked over to my dresser, where Jeremy, Bea, and Anna's gifts sat.

I got Anna a Yankees baseball cap since she would not shut up about how badly she wanted one. I asked my dad to make a special stop on his way home from work today to get Jeremy's present from the city. Bea's present I had found in her favorite gift shop here in town. She was hard to shop for, and I wanted my gift to be perfect. Over these last few months, she had become so important to me. I wanted my gift to show her that. I wanted it to tell her that I knew what mattered most to her and that it mattered to me too.

Joel: *You drive me nuts! See you soon! Xo*

Bea: *I can't wait to see you too! Xo*

A few days ago, we went to see Peter together to wish him a Merry Christmas. Bea had baked cookies for him and brought him a Christmas flower arrangement. I brought him a framed picture of him, Bea, and me that we had taken the month before out at the pond. He had loved all of it, tears forming in his blue eyes when he opened the photo. He thanked us, and he and Tess gave us gifts that she had gotten at some store called Barneys. I received a very nice tie with ducks on it (Peter's idea), and Bea had received a beautiful ring that had cost a small fortune. Peter had said a girl so beautiful inside and out deserved something equally as lovely. I agreed completely.

I put the wrapped gifts into my backpack and went to knock on Anna's door. I could smell her perfume from the hallway, and I did our secret code knock.

"Anna?" I called from outside her door.

"Come in," she sang from within.

I opened the door to find Anna sitting at her vanity table, applying some lipstick. Justin Bieber's new album was playing from her speaker.

"Hey, I'm almost ready," she said, looking at me in the mirror. "You have the gifts?"

"Yeah, you got yours?" I said.

"Right there." She pointed to a large shopping bag that read Macy's on the side. "I hope they like my gifts! Bea is really hard to shop for. Jer, on the other hand, is super easy."

"Yeah, just get Jer a gift card to Starbucks, and he's the happiest guy in the world."

"The man loves his coffee," Anna agreed. She got up and grabbed her bag from the bed. "Alright, let's go!"

We walked down the street and could see the Canning's Christmas lights lighting up their home, not too far away. Anna and I sang Christmas carols while we walked, throwing snowballs at each other the whole way.

We did not knock when we got there, just went right in as we'd come to do. Michael Bublé Christmas music played inside, and the whole house smelled like delicious food. On the coffee table in the living room, there was an assortment of chips, cookies, baguette with salmon and cream cheese, and some nice cheese and crackers.

Jeremy emerged from the kitchen with four cups of hot chocolate, somehow balancing in his arms, and he saw us and grinned. "Hey, guys, you're here! I thought I'd play housewife and make us some *ordoovras*." He pronounced hors d'œuvres incorrectly on purpose like the American teenager he was.

"You did all this, Jer?" Anna asked as she took off her coat, and I hung it in the closet with mine.

"No, he definitely made the hot chocolate, though," Bea said, coming out behind Jeremy.

"It's instant," Jeremy said with a shrug.

"Bea, this is so nice!" Anna said, clapping. She and I came into the living room as Jeremy struggled to set down the mugs.

"So, we have lots of yummy stuff. I recommend the gouda since it's my favorite," Bea said, pointing to the cheese tray. I smiled to myself, thinking, *there she goes talking about food again.*

Jeremy had sprawled out on the couch, still leaving room for Bea to sit down next to him. Anna perched herself on the big red armchair, and I sat on the footstool at the end of it. I noticed that

Bea was wearing a red knit dress and small snowflake earrings. I could not help but smile every time I saw her. If it was not her cute Christmas spirit, it was something else.

Jeremy grabbed a piece of baguette with salmon on it and took a big bite. I noticed there were a few small gifts on the table, some wrapped in pretty gold paper, some messily wrapped in red with multiple bows. It was easy to know which ones were Bea's and which were Jeremy's.

We talked and ate for a while, almost to the end of the Michael Bublé album, but before long, Anna could not wait any longer for presents. We began exchanging gifts, laughing, thanking each other, and having a great time. Jeremy got me socks with burgers on them, fitting enough because I had Dad pick up a Wahlburger and fries earlier that day as Jer's gift. He burst into laughter and dug in right there, saying, "Great gift, man."

I kept Bea's present in my pocket, wanting to pull her aside to give it to her. No one seemed to notice, and Bea was too polite to say anything when I did not seem to have anything for her. She must have decided it would be best to keep her gift for me a secret too. I just smiled to myself, feeling the tiny box in my sweater pocket.

We finished as much food as we could, Jeremy eating most of it, and Anna and I helped him and Bea bring the dishes and leftovers into the kitchen. We all cleaned up together, as Anna and I knew where most things were in the Canning's kitchen. When we were done, I texted Anna to take Jeremy somewhere so Bea and I could be alone.

"Hey Jer, you still have to show me your fast food napkin collection!" Anna said enthusiastically. "You have one from every burger joint in the state, right?" I had to keep from laughing at the sarcasm I could hear in Anna's voice. But it was effective. Jer's eyes lit up with excitement, and he jumped off the island barstool. "Yeah, I do! Come on. I'll show you!"

The two of them went off to Jeremy's room, leaving me alone with Bea. She was just finishing drying a serving bowl, and I suddenly felt nervous about my plan. I was bursting with excitement. I had been planning this moment for weeks. Ready or not, I was going for it.

"Hey Bea, want to check out the stars with me?" I asked, my voice steady as the rest of me vibrated with adrenaline. She set the bowl back into the cupboard and turned around to face me. "Yeah, sure, we can sit on the front porch."

I followed her to the foyer, and we got our coats on in comfortable silence. The night was cold and clear. We could see our breath, and the sky was sparkling with stars. Just as I had hoped, the crescent moon was out, resting above us like a guardian. We sat on the swing at the edge of the porch, pushing it gently back and forth with our feet.

"Do you remember when we first met?" I asked.

"Yes, of course," Bea answered. "You almost died."

"Well, for me, something else happened that moment. I was suddenly open to something new, something I've never felt before."

"And what's that?"

"It was a sense of feeling whole, I guess . . . complete. Like I'd been missing something my whole life but just didn't know it until then."

Bea was silent, staring at me with her big, blue eyes. They almost looked navy in the night. I was so nervous, and my mind was racing like a horse around a track.

"You had been what was missing," I said, finally. Then I pulled out the little white box from my pocket and handed it to her. "Merry Christmas, Bea."

She took the box in her slender hands and untied the ribbon. She opened it and peered inside. It was a silver necklace, and the pendant had a photo of a moon.

"This is the moon that is looking down on us right now," I explained. "December twentieth."

Bea looked up at the moon in the sky and then back at the small box.

"It's the moon that is looking down on us the night I finally tell you...that I'm in love with you."

Bea stared up at me, her face expressionless until a smile broke across it. "You love me?"

"Yes." I put my hand to her face, gently brushing a curl out of the way.

"So maybe this will be the moon that is looking down on us the night you finally kiss me," she said.

I laughed, and then she laughed too. I turned toward her, and her body followed. Leaning in slowly, I let my instincts guide me.

My lips brushed against hers, and I felt electric shocks move through me. I felt a rush of warmth, my body suddenly feeling like water. I did not know a kiss could be like that.

The four of us walked together down the icy road toward Suicide Hill, which was the big hill our neighborhood had nicknamed down at the end of the street. Anna and I were so excited as the snow crunched noisily underneath our boots. As we walked, Jeremy and I swapped places, so he could tease my sister, who was slightly scared, as she had no idea what tubing was going to be like.

Bea and Jeremy had shown us some pictures in an album before we left the house. Both Jeremy and Bea had rosy cheeks and looked exhilarated, their hats lopsided on top of their heads, both holding onto a giant inflatable doughnut. *What had I gotten myself into?* I wondered with an inward smile.

We all ran up the steep hill, out of breath, and tremendously thrilled to fly down for the first time. Bea pulled my arm and shoved me onto the black snow tube as she jumped on, and we flew down the hill. I felt the freezing cold air whip my face, and I recognized my voice screaming from the exciting adrenaline-charged feeling of speeding into the dark unknown.

Next, I could hear Anna and Jeremy going down on their tube, shrieking happily.

"Oh, my God! That was amazing. Let's do it again!" Anna cried out in delight. And in one swift movement, she and Jeremy were leaning into the crisp night air, shielding their faces with one hand from the freezing cold and trying to hold onto the tube with the other as they went back up.

Bea and I went back up too. I had no idea how extremely hard it was to control the tube and the direction you are going. It is a mystery that everyone does not sustain life-threatening or severe injuries from this crazy activity. Halfway up the hill, I heard Anna singing a goofy Christmas carol that I remembered from our childhood, and once we reached the top of the hill, I looked up at the night sky. I could still see the moon on Bea's necklace, and I could not believe I had finally told her. I didn't need her to say it back right away, but it felt incredible just knowing that I'd finally told her how I felt and that when I kissed her, she kissed me back. All I wanted to do was take her somewhere, just us, and kiss her some more.

As we walked up the big hill, Bea was very quiet, and I could see her shivering beside me. It was colder than I had thought. I secretly loved the crisp air and the cold and did not miss California one bit. Winter in this place made me feel so alive and vital.

"I'm going to go down with Jer. Why don't you take Anna down with you? This one's faster!" she said, giving me a devilish grin.

"So, what did Bea think of her gift? Did she love it?" Anna asked once it was just us standing on the hill.

I smiled, remembering the pretty much single greatest moment of my life. "Yeah, she did."

"What I wouldn't do to find a guy who felt this way about me." Her breath trailed off into the cold air. "I've probably watched way too many romantic movies," Anna continued. "Or maybe I'm being influenced by you, but the idea of finding someone who loves me the way Dad loves Mom kind of scares me. Mom is so amazing. I'm just, well, just me. You know?"

"You're amazing, Anna," I replied. "What about that guy you keep texting . . . Eric? He's in your music class, isn't he?"

Anna grinned at me as she replied, "Eric? Eric who?"

We had gone up and down the hill several times when I noticed Bea whispering something frantically into Jeremy's ear. I figured she had something up her sleeve at first until I recognized the look of fear register upon Jeremy's face. He put his arm around Bea and gave her a gentle squeeze, whispered back to her, and then turned back toward Anna and me. I caught Bea wiping her face with her sleeve before turning around, a fake-looking smile turning her lips up ever so slightly.

"Is everything okay, guys?" I asked tentatively, hoping not to be meddling in some family thing.

"Sure. We're just feeling a bit whooped. You guys wanna call it a night? I think we are going to start walking back. Maybe we can try a movie night tomorrow. I am dying to see a good shoot 'em up." Jeremy smiled comfortably and looked back toward his sister. "Come on, Sis. My feet are getting more numb by the second."

Bea walked past us, her smile fading a little too quickly.

I thought I noticed her favoring one side a little as she walked.

"Are you sure you're okay, Bea? Did you hurt yourself going down?"

"Nope, everything's perfect. That was a blast!" she added hurriedly. "What did you guys think of it? That was your first time, right?"

"It was amazing. It felt just like going down a crazy water slide in a tube. My parents used to take us to this amazing outdoor waterpark, Splish Splash. It was the best!" I said.

We exchanged hugs and high fives and promised to pick out a thriller for the next evening. Anna and I invited them to our place for a change, and Jeremy begged Anna to make him her famous guacamole.

Once back home, thawed and warmed up, Anna headed off to bed with a tired grin, her dark curls matted down on one side of her head. I was feeling so lucky and blessed. I had the best family and the best friends and now the best girlfriend in the world.

I could not wait to quiet my mind and think about Bea. What a kiss. I had kissed a few girls before as a young teenager and my very first girlfriend during my sophomore year. Nothing had prepared me for the feelings that kissing Bea brought out in me. I changed into a pair of sweatpants and a tee shirt and slipped under my blanket, grateful to be out of the chilly wind and excited for the morning. I thought about the amazing night we had all had and reached for my journal.

December 20

I kissed my future wife tonight, and it was more magical than I could have ever imagined. I didn't know lips could be that soft or a moment so sweet.

My fatigue from all the climbing caught up with me, and I slipped away with thoughts of Bea swirling around in my mind, my heart aching with equal amounts of desire and love.

I jolted awake and sat up with a start. I grabbed my phone beside me, knocking over my journal. It was 2:22 a.m. I felt sick, nauseous. I had a feeling of foreboding that I could not shake. I lay back and tried to think of Bea and let thoughts of her lull me back to sleep. Even though my eyes were closed, I could see car lights flashing past in the distance. The night remained still and calm, with only the faint whistle of the wind making winter sounds outside my window. As I began drifting off, I thought about the anxious feelings in my body and suddenly realized the lights must have been from a passing ambulance. I said a silent prayer for whoever might have been in trouble this beautiful winter's night and then turned over and began to fall back asleep despite the feelings of trepidation coursing through me.

The feeling intensified, and suddenly a thought entered my mind. *Bea.* I grabbed for my phone once again and texted Bea. I waited impatiently for her to text back. Next, I texted Jeremy. I was hoping I would not hear back from either of them, and when my phone pinged softly, my heart stopped in my chest, and a cold sweat broke out on my skin.

"Dude, we're heading to the hospital. Bea's sick. Can't get into it now."

I did not reply and instead grabbed my jeans and a hoody off my bed and ran downstairs two at a time, nearly falling down the last few steps. I stuffed my bare feet into my boots, grabbed the keys, and flew out the door. In one fast movement, I swiped the snow off the front windshield with one arm and jumped into the SUV, jamming the keys into the ignition as fast as I could. I tried not to think of all the possibilities. I tried to calm my breathing as I inhaled the cold and drove the five minutes to the hospital.

Once inside, I looked around frantically but did not see the Cannings. I pulled out my phone and texted Jeremy.

Joel: *I'm here. Where are you?*

I wanted to scream while I waited for what seemed like an eternity. Finally, I heard the faint ping of my phone.

Jeremy: *Floor 3, ICU.*

Oh, God. ICU. I remembered too well the acronym for the Intensive Care Unit.

I was stone sober as I rushed forward to the elevator and emerged on the third floor.

Ria was crying softly in Brandon's arms, while Jeremy stood guiltily staring out the window. I slowed my steps and stopped. I did not know my life was about to change forever, but somehow there was a part of me that had known somehow. Jeremy noticed me in the reflection of the window.

"Hey," he whispered. It looked like he had been crying.

Oh, my God. What could have happened? I was suddenly more scared than I had ever been in my life, and I fought overwhelming nausea that threatened to suffocate me as I breathed the antiseptic smell in the hallway. Ria and Brandon turned and sat down beside one another. I approached them and leaned down to offer Ria a hug.

"What's going on? What happened to Bea? Where is she? Can I see her?" I stammered all at once.

Ria looked up wearily and said, "I'm so sorry, Joel. You will have to ask Bea. We promised."

Sometime before the morning dawned, a nurse shook me awake.

"Are you Joel Peterson?" she asked sweetly. I looked around and saw that the Cannings were not there.

"Yes," I said, slowly rising.

"Miss Bea is awake and asking for you."

CHAPTER SEVEN

I followed the nurse down the hallway, where worried family members sat nervously waiting for news about their loved ones. Some were crying, others prayed softly or talked quietly into their phones, while others chewed on their fingernails, frantic with worry.

"Joel, we've moved Bea out of ICU for now. She is in 307 on the left. Please do not stay too long, as she needs lots of rest. She's got a big day ahead of her," the kind nurse continued.

"Thank you." I saw Ria sitting outside room 307.

She looked up and offered me a genuine smile. "We wanted to let you sleep. Jeremy and his father went home to take a shower and bring back some breakfast." She went on, "I know you must feel pretty confused right now, and I'm sorry if we've caused you any upset. It is not an easy situation. Bea would like to explain, dear. Go on in." She looked back at the magazine that was open and upside down in her lap.

I stopped a few steps before reaching the door and did my best to compose myself before entering. I heard the loud beeping of a machine and looked inside. Bea was alone in the room, lying in a hospital bed. Her eyes were closed, and her blood pressure cuff was busy measuring her blood pressure on one side while an IV dripped and droned on her other side, the long tubes disappearing into needles in her veins. Her hair was in ringlets on either side of her face. She looked so peaceful. I could not imagine what could be wrong with her. I quickly scanned what I could see of her body, and it did not look as though she was hurt, as there were no bandages or bruises visible.

Bea opened her eyes suddenly and offered a small smile. "Hey."

I leaned over her, kissing her forehead gently. "How are you feeling?"

"I've felt better and worse. Umm, did my mom or dad tell you anything?"

I shook my head.

"I . . . ."

A team of doctors walked in, Ria following behind. "Miss Canning! Good morning my dear! We were hoping we wouldn't be seeing you so soon, especially around the holidays." The doctor who seemed in charge gestured for his entourage to gather around. "As you know, Bea, we are a teaching hospital. Do you have any objections?"

"No, Doctor Stevens. I know the drill," Bea replied, sneaking in an apprehensive look at me and looking for her mother, as if for moral support.

"And who do we have here?" Dr. Stevens met my gaze, his eyebrow raised in interest.

"Hey, uh, I'm Joel," I said. "Bea's . . . boyfriend." I reached for her delicate hand and gave her a gentle squeeze. I watched her face relax, and she took a big breath, as though she had been holding on to it for a long time.

"Bea, is it okay if we proceed?" he inquired, looking at me as I stood there, two feet planted firmly on the ground with no intention of moving an inch.

"Yes." She squeezed my hand and held on tightly, as if afraid that what I would soon learn would separate us.

"Bea Canning has a diagnosis of stage-four autoimmune hepatitis. She presented with less than 7 percent of her liver at age fifteen and underwent several biopsies and extensive treatment with many medications. Her liver is very stubborn and is not responding to treatment. We will keep her here for monitoring and to stabilize her ALT and ASTs, as well as get her in for both an MRI and CT scan, another biopsy, and ultrasound."

They continued in their doctor jargon, the doctor in charge asking the interested students many questions. I wished I knew what this was all about. I felt sick. Stage four anything did not sound very good. Hepatitis? Wasn't that a fatal condition that addicts got from sharing needles?

The doctor continued checking Bea's vitals, asking the medical students questions. He then assured Bea she was in the best of hands before shaking Ria's hand, giving me a nod, and then leaving with his entourage to continue his rounds.

"I'll leave the two of you alone, honey." Ria gave me another kind smile and left the room as well.

"What was all that about?" I asked, completely unnerved.

"It's a long story. You sure you're up for this?"

"As long as it has to do with you, I'm up for it. You can't scare me away that easily."

Hearing my own voice, I thought I sounded as different from how I felt as possible. Inside, my stomach roiled with upset, my heart was beating way too quickly, and my head was spinning faster than I was comfortable with. I closed my eyes and urged my thoughts to stop long enough for Bea to realize I could be counted on to share this moment.

Bea went into the story of how a few years ago, she had slowly stopped eating and how it went unnoticed for a couple of months. Her mom had been working as a realtor in those days and was often busy showing clients homes during the dinner hour. So, she had hired a nanny to cook dinner and help Bea and Jeremy with their homework. As time went on, Ria was becoming more and more frustrated as she began noticing that much of the fresh produce was needing to be thrown out because it was not getting eaten. Jeremy had a healthy appetite for junk food, and Bea had always preferred and enjoyed fresh produce, which had a short shelf life.

Then one day, Bea and Jeremy had been at the mall with Ria, and she noticed the whites of Bea's eyes had seemed off like there was a yellow tinge to them. A few days before, Ria had taken Bea to their family doctor because Bea had been acting more tired than normal and had seemed to have little appetite. The doctor had said something about how it sounded as though she might have possibly contracted a mild form of hepatitis A from contaminated tap water.

The doctor had ordered some blood work to be done and said she would follow up with them the following day if she was correct and would prescribe some antibiotics immediately. As the story often goes, the doctor had, unfortunately, come down with a bad cold and had gone home early and missed the following day, and as the following day was a Friday, Bea and her test results had fallen through the cracks.

Ria had a bad feeling while they walked around the mall and decided they should leave to take Bea to the local hospital. She was admitted right away, and this was where she had remained for a week with no diagnosis forthcoming. The staff had seemed stumped over her condition, and by this time, she had turned completely yellow.

"I looked like a banana!" Bea shared. "It was very frustrating. They used me like a pincushion and continued talking as though they knew what they were doing until they finally admitted defeat. Mom really helped, as she got more and more upset with their inability to diagnose me. She's my hero!" Bea smiled at the door where her mom sat waiting.

After a week of inconclusive tests and a rapidly worsening patient, Bea was transferred to Dell Children's Hospital, which is one of the best hospitals in the U.S. She was transferred by ambulance with Ria while Brandon and Jeremy drove behind them. Ria never left her side and had been allowed to remain with her in the same room.

As soon as Bea arrived, a team of confident doctors delivered her diagnosis. It was autoimmune hepatitis type 1. Basically, this meant that she had less than 7 percent of her liver functioning. The rest of it had died. I further learned from Bea that the liver could not regenerate once it is cirrhotic. Once this happens, the only option is keeping the 7 percent functioning with an intensive treatment of medicines, which cause other severe problems and possibly fatal outcomes. I was stunned into silence as I listened to her tell me the entire story.

"You mean to tell me you almost died?" I asked her bluntly.

"Yeah. I almost did. It was just over two years ago. I was there for a month. I take a lot of medication, and it makes me feel awful most of the time. But we are dealing with things, and things could be a lot worse, so I feel pretty lucky and grateful to all the great doctors."

I remembered the way the hospital staff seemed to know Bea and her family the day Peter was hospitalized after his fall, and it all came together and made a lot of sense.

"So, what does this mean? Why are you here now? What happened on the hill last night?"

"I just overdid it, I guess. I have not been feeling too well lately. My liver kind of hurt. That is a bad sign. And I had a fever. I must be careful about a lot of things. All the meds I take cause secondary diseases like osteoporosis and other fun things. The bottom line, Joel, is that I'm probably going to need a liver transplant someday." Bea turned her head away from me as her voice broke on that last word.

I was stunned. I searched my brain for signs that Bea was not well. I remembered thinking she was tired a lot and just thought she liked to stay up late, like most teenagers. Now that I thought about it, I also recalled her missing a lot of school and talking about many outings she would have planned with her mom in the city.

I had so many questions, but I did not want to overwhelm Bea with my worry. I wanted to be strong for her, someone she can rely on to help her. I was still reeling with the shock of what I was learning, but I knew I would have the time to sort through my thoughts later. I looked outside the window and noticed the snow was blowing sideways. A blizzard, I thought.

"Ho! Ho! Ho!" A man wearing a Santa costume walked past, jingling his bells. It was only a few days until Christmas, and I began wondering what would be in store in the coming days. I thought of all the people in the hospital, most of whom would remain here for the holiday. I felt a wave of sadness wash over me.

"Do you know how long you'll be in here?" I asked hesitantly.

"Not yet," she said sadly. "We'll know more after the biopsy later today. Not my favorite way to spend my day. But hey, why don't you head home and take a little time to yourself. I'm sure those chairs down the hall weren't the best, and you look like you need some rest."

Her lovely smile disarmed me, and I felt the first sting of tears begin to form in my eyes. I quickly blinked before they could appear and forced a laugh. "Okay, I'll grab a shower and check in on Peter and then be back around lunch." I leaned down and gently kissed her pale cheek and whispered, "I love you."

I made my way down the hall, the noises and movement around me echoing faintly in the distance, as though I was in a strange dream. My heart felt like it had stopped, and I wondered if maybe I was just dreaming, and none of this was happening. The word *how* replayed over and over in my brain.

"Joel?"

I stopped and recognized Ria coming toward me, a sheepish look on her face. She hugged me. "I'm sorry, dear. We all promised to live life as normally as we can and not make Bea feel different all the time. This illness has robbed her of so much. She's been through so much," her voice trailed off, emotion replacing her determination to remain brave.

I could see the deep worry and strain on her face now. I wondered how I did not see it before. In fact, thinking back to past dinners and other times we all spent time together, I could now recall the sobering looks between them, as if they were constantly being reminded that every smile was not supposed to reach its full potential. Bea's mere presence was a constant reminder that life was precarious. I did not have anywhere near a full picture of the situation yet, and I did not know if it was fair or if I should. I decided I would not ask questions or seek out information. It is not like this changed anything for me. If anything, I loved Bea even more and would be at her side no matter what happened.

After driving home, I sat in the driveway, turned off the ignition, and watched the snow fall. It had died down a little, and I watched as intermittent white snowflakes landed on the windshield. I leaned forward and discovered the intricacy of each feathery ice crystal displaying delicate and perfect symmetry. I had heard there were no two snowflakes alike and had always been amazed by this. They were tiny ice crystals that come together to form one snowflake. As they tumbled through the air, swirling and spiraling, they looked so beautiful, each taking a different path to the ground and landing in its own unique shape. I used to have a hard time believing this was possible, but today, I accepted this as fact.

Bea was like a snowflake: unique, fragile, exquisite, and utterly flawed and perfect at the same time. Born of a raindrop, laced by the cold, spinning through space and dancing through trees, snowflakes, like Bea, were a reminder of all that we are, of how fragile it all was.

Once inside my house, I dropped onto the couch and closed my eyes. Christmas music playing softly in the living room, and the emotion of the past twenty-four hours came tumbling down.

"Joel?" One look at me and my mom knew there was something wrong. "Where were you? Is everything okay, honey?"

I remained slumped on the couch while I let my heart pour out to my mom. She listened intently, taking a sudden intake of breath when I said the words liver disease and transplant in the same sentence as Bea's name. My mom was a pillar of strength, no matter what happens to anyone in her life. She had the biggest heart and never ran out of compassion. She would give the shirt off her back, give her last dollar, whether she knew the person or not. I tried to emulate her while growing up and tried to listen intently to others when they spoke. It was truly a gift she had, making her seem like the best conversationalist even though she had not opened her mouth once. She never disappointed, however, and I felt like she understood the situation completely.

"Let us know how we can help. Anything," she said when I was done.

"Thanks, Mom. I am going to take a shower and close my eyes for a few minutes and head back to the hospital. And Mom, thanks for always being there for me."

I hurried up the stairs, suddenly eager to be alone.

"Whoa! What's the rush, loser?" Anna jokingly shoved me gently.

"Hey, Sis." I hurried past her, allowing her comment to bounce off me.

When I heard the click of my door shutting, I slipped to the ground and felt the blood turn cold in my body. It felt like electric shocks were dancing in my head, and I felt overwhelmingly tired and anxious at the same time. As my thoughts threatened to bury me in sorrow, I let myself give way to a few racking, silent sobs.

I suddenly felt a wave of anger burst through my cloud of grief. Bea had this sad look on her face whenever I spoke of my travel plans or going to Stanford next fall. Like she knew the entire time, she did not have the same options I had. Did she try to tell me? I wondered. Was there something I missed? How could I not have known? I realized that I did know. I knew something but was so caught up in my feelings for her that I missed it. I felt like such an idiot.

Even though I just wanted to crawl under a rock, I decided to write instead.

December 21

My world not only shattered today, but my life has taken on a new meaning. From now on, I want to dedicate my life to making Bea's life the best it can be. All I want is to love her each and every day.

CHAPTER EIGHT

In a burst of emotion, I jumped up and ran downstairs. My mom and dad were sitting together on the sofa, deep in conversation. When they saw me, they immediately stopped talking and looked in my direction.

"Joel," said my dad in a serious tone. "I'm so sorry. Your mother just told me about Bea. Is there anything we can do?"

"I don't think so. I will know more later. I am going to check on Peter and then make my way back to the hospital. I will call later. But Dad, Mom, thanks."

"Of course, honey." My mom stood and hugged me, her eyes glossy with tears. I hugged her back tightly, feeling helpless in this situation I suddenly found myself in. Yesterday morning all I was worried about was if Bea would kiss me back. I felt so guilty now to realize she had much bigger problems to worry about. I said goodbye to my parents and went to get my coat and boots on. On my way out, Anna caught me in the stairwell near the front foyer.

"Mom told me. Is she going to be okay?"

I looked at her soberly and replied, "I don't know. I think she's pretty sick."

"I'm so sorry, Joel. I didn't see this coming."

"I know, me neither."

"What does that mean for you?"

"It doesn't change the way I feel about her. Just means we'll have bigger obstacles than I thought." I felt sick with anxiety, and I just wanted to be next to Bea again, there for whatever she needed. Anna nodded, knowing that my mind was set. I could see how sad this made her, but still, she gave me a hug. We did not hug often. My sister was small, and she wrapped her arms around me gently, as if she thought I might break under too much pressure.

"Maybe you can come with me to the hospital to visit her tomorrow or something," I suggested.

"Sure. That would be good. Please give her a hug for me."

I smiled at her appreciatively.

I found Peter sitting in a high-backed burgundy velvet chair in the main lobby. He had told me once that he enjoys watching people coming and going. As I walked toward him, I was thinking of how unfair and fragile life was. Here was Peter, eighty-six years old, still a vital, intelligent, loving man with lots of money, a wife he loves, beautiful homes and cars, and he is stuck here because he had fallen through the cracks.

As I thought this, another thought entered my mind. Neither Bea nor I would have ever gotten to know Peter had it not been for misfortune. If he had not needed Bea's help, they never would have developed such an endearing friendship.

I had learned when I talked to Peter that he and Tess met much later in life, in their forties. They had never had children, which I think is why they felt such joy from their relationship with Bea. She was more like their granddaughter, but only because of the age difference. In fact, it was truly incredible how close they were. Both Bea and Peter had told me on separate occasions that they considered the other their closest friend. Peter made Bea laugh harder than I had ever known her to laugh. She even seemed to have a special smile she reserved just for him. I imagined it being extremely hard on Peter knowing about Bea's illness.

"Hey Peter, how are you feeling?" I sat down beside him and noticed the bruises had turned from dark purple to yellowish-green.

"I'm feeling perfect, of course. Never better. Don't you think my bruises bring out the blue in my eyes?" he joked. "Where's my Bea?" He looked toward the front door as if he expected her to walk in any moment. His smile faded, and he looked quickly in my direction, a question upon his crinkled face.

"I'm sorry, Peter. Bea was rushed to the hospital last night."

Peter instinctively reached out his hand toward mine and held on tight. I had never felt a softer hand next to Bea's. It felt shiny like his skin was made from some special silky material laid overtop old, tired bones. I did not want to look up and see the pain on his face, so I continued staring at his hand, scattered with lines and sunspots.

He braced himself before asking, "How is she?"

"I'll learn more soon. It sounded as though they had a long day planned for her. Bea made me promise to come see you before I head back over."

"So, you know?"

"Yes, I know. I do not really understand much yet, but I wanted to give her some space, you know. She looked really pale and tired, but she was still smiling like her usual self when I left the hospital a few hours ago."

"Bea is an angel sent from heaven. I cannot understand how I've gone through most of my life without her. When I found out she was sick . . . ," Peter's voice trailed off as he shook his head sadly.

"Did you know," he continued with a slight smile, "that Bea and I met in the hospital? I had gone in to have my gallbladder removed, and I looked up one day, and there she was, sharing my room with me. The hospital was overcrowded, and they had no choice but to put us in the same room together. It only lasted a few hours, but even though she had just had a nasty biopsy procedure completed, she was concerned for me. She looked over and told me a joke." Peter began laughing. "It was the worst joke I'd ever heard, but she told it so sweetly, she could have been reading me a shopping list, and it would have been music to my ears. Would you like to know what the joke was?"

"Sure."

"She asked me, 'Did you hear about the guy who lost his whole left side?' and I said, 'No, how is he?' and she replied, 'He's alright now.' "

Peter erupted into laughter. For a minute, I pictured the scene he described, and then my smile grew bigger and bigger until I began to laugh as well. The two of us sat there laughing as people stared, and tears grew in our eyes until I remembered the situation, and I stopped. Peter reached into his sweater pocket and pulled out a crisp white hanky with his initials monogrammed on it and wiped his watery eyes.

The two of us sat there together, sharing our favorite moments being with Bea with one another. Peter obviously knew all too well the severity of the situation and was honoring his friendship with Bea by not discussing matters with me. Instead, Peter began talking about his country property, describing the landscape, the two stocked ponds, and the trees that had been imported from all around the world.

"I'd like to have the two of you over for a weekend, once I can walk out of here."

"Soon," I said with a smile.

Peter leaned over and patted my hand. "Son, you'd better go see how Bea is doing, and please let her know old Peter is thinking of her, and I'll have some new jokes to share with her the next time we see one another."

"Thank you, Peter. Will do. Please give Tess our best, and we'll come by again on Christmas just as we planned."

"Excellent," Peter said, leaning back in his chair and closing his eyes with contentment. I left him and made my way back to Bea, who had just texted me.

Bea: *I miss you.*

When I got to the hospital, I stopped in the gift shop to buy some flowers and a little stuffed bear. I went up to Bea's room on the third floor to find that she was sleeping soundly. The color of her skin had changed from a flushed pink to a pale yellow. Her jaundiced look took my breath away, and fear fought its way into my lungs, cutting off my breath. I slowly approached her bed, noticing her slightly parted lips. The machines hummed and whirred on either side of her, a reminder of the cruelty of the situation.

I quietly placed the flowers on the small bedside table and carefully tucked the bear in beside her. I just stood there staring at her and wondering how I'd lived my entire life up until only a few months ago without her in it. She had to be okay. I closed my eyes and prayed with everything I had in me and then softly whispered in her small delicate ear, "It doesn't change anything between us, Bea. I will love you forever."

Bea made it home for Christmas Eve with her medication adjusted and her condition stable. She had a little bit less of her liver, and her energy was depleted, yet she still had a smile that could light up a room.

I went to pick her up from the hospital and bring her home so that the rest of the Cannings could get the surprise ready. I had brought her some clothes that Ria had picked out, a pair of black pants and a white knit sweater. I could tell she was happy to be wearing something other than pajamas. Even though it had been just days, I think it felt like she had been in the hospital for weeks to all of us.

Peter could not wait to see Bea. I had called him earlier in the day to tell him she would be coming home and to confirm our plans for Christmas Day. We were going to visit him and Tess with some cookies and cake and exchange gifts before we would go to our respective family dinners.

I knew Peter and Tess did not have any family but each other, not having any children and all, but I didn't think they minded too much. They had each other, and they had us and some other wonderful friends their own age. Peter had said they were hosting a dinner at the retirement home with some of their oldest friends and catering from the fancy French bistro in town. I think Peter was very much looking forward to putting on a suit and entertaining with good company. It had been so long since anything special like that had happened in his life.

I had splurged on a bottle of his favorite red wine as his Christmas present to enjoy with his guests at their big dinner. Bea had gotten him a pair of suspenders from his favorite haberdashery shop, a soft lilac color which was his favorite, and then we had split the cost of a fine straw fedora with the same lilac-colored band. It even came in a hatbox, which Bea had said he would greatly appreciate.

On the way back to Bea's house, I played the local Christmas station on the radio, and she hummed along, enjoying the view out the window.

"I bet you're looking forward to sleeping in your own bed," I said, grabbing her hand from her lap and lacing our fingers together.

"Yeah, I am. Just excited to start feeling normal again. Or at least pretending I'm normal again," she said with a laugh.

I was still processing everything and trying to understand all the technicalities of her condition. It was a lot to understand and think about. Everything I had been excited to experience with her now had her illness looming over it. I grasped that there were things she could not do or places she could not go. She needed to be close to her team of doctors, and she could not go to third world countries because of the different bacteria and climate. I was scared to ask what else would be different about our future than I had been planning.

As hard as it was to accept these new obstacles, I still stood by the fact that it did not change anything for me. This was the girl I wanted to be with, sick or not.

When we arrived at the Canning's home, it was just getting dark out, and the house was lit up with lights. There was an inflatable Santa at the mouth of the driveway to welcome us, along with a big sign that Anna, Jeremy, and I had made that said in bold red letters, "WELCOME HOME BEA!"

Bea's face lit up as we drove up to the house. "Where did that Santa come from?" she asked with a laugh.

"Your dad went out and bought it the other day. Jer and I helped him set it up."

"And the sign?"

"Anna, Jer, and I did that. You like it?"

"You guys are so awesome," she said, squeezing my hand.

I grabbed her bag from the backseat, and we went in. Bea was shocked when she found that it looked like Santa's workshop inside her home. There were lights and garlands everywhere, and stockings were hung over the fireplace, Christmas music played, and her family was waiting around a giant Christmas tree overloaded with gifts.

"Welcome home, Bea," they all said at once when she walked in the door.

"You guys are amazing," she said. "It looks amazing!"

After a wonderful hour of remembering and sharing fond memories from the past, everyone seemed to notice all at once that Bea started looking tired.

"Mom, is it okay if Joel tucks me in?" she asked with a yawn.

"Sure, honey." She walked toward Bea and extended her arms for a hug. "Merry Christmas, my darling!"

Bea went around the room and hugged everyone, and I noticed the tense yet relieved look on her family's faces.

Once inside her cute blue room, I waited on the edge of her bed while she got ready for bed in the bathroom. I'd never spent much time in her room, and this was the first time I'd gotten a good look around. My eyes locked onto a framed picture of her, Peter, and her family. I took in the mirrored bedside desk, mini crystal chandelier, and the full-length standing jewelry cabinet with a mirror. I ran my hands across her cotton duvet, featuring an elegant floral motif in blush pink and as soft and enchanting as she was.

She walked shyly out of her en suite bathroom, wearing a fluffy cream robe with roses on it. Our eyes locked together. I noticed the whites of her eyes were tinged yellow, and the rims of her eyes were red with fatigue and strain.

I pulled down her covers. "Get in here, you."

I wanted to cuddle her and keep her safe from the world. The problem was that the world seemed like a kinder place than her own body. Bea lay her head down and sighed as she shivered. I lay down beside her and took her hand in mine as we enjoyed the quiet with only the wind whistling outside her bedroom window.

The faint sound of Christmas carols could be heard coming from down the hall. Bea was holding her necklace in her other hand when she suddenly jerked her body. "Joel, I forgot my gift for you. It's in there." She motioned to the drawer of her desk.

I reached over and pulled open the drawer and found a beautiful gold-wrapped gift inside. I smiled at her and carefully pulled open the paper. It was an old-world leather-wrapped embossed journal with Amalfi paper. On the front, words had been embossed in fine cursive: Joel Peterson, Author.

December 24

These past few days have not been easy. My world has been forever changed. But from the struggle comes the good, which is a new closeness I have with the girl I love. She is flawed, beautiful, and enigmatic. She has touched me in ways I had yet to discover. I want nothing less than forever with her. Merry Christmas, Bea. It's you and me now.

CHAPTER NINE

The winter flew by as if the bitter wind had carried our lives with its currents and released us once the birds were ready to welcome us to spring. It was a wonderful time of relaxation, laughter, and most importantly, love. Bea and I saw each other every day, even if it was only for a few minutes. I learned so much about her dreams for the future and about her past. The story of how she had dealt with her new reality among friends, at school, and within her own mind impacted me in a way that changed me forever.

Bea talked as if a flood gate had opened, and I listened.

"When I first was diagnosed, I remained in the hospital for over a month," Bea told me. "I felt like a human pin cushion as nurses and doctors were forever needing blood for more tests and to try new intravenous medicines. They eventually ran out of places to prick and had to use my feet for the IV. I was a rainbow of colors from the bruises that formed on my body. One of the two scariest things for me was the looks on the faces of my parents and brother when they were at my side. My mom never left me and had a special bed made up in my room. Sometimes, I heard her crying, and once she left in the middle of the night, and I heard her sobbing in the empty room beside us. I had never seen my mother cry. Only when our one-eyed dog, Mandy, died had I seen tears in her eyes.

The other thing that scared me was the feeling of my life careening out of control. Thoughts of plans I had for my future, places I wanted to visit, things I wanted to do, all seemed so out of reach now, as my body continued to fail me. I wondered if I would see my next birthday.

When I got out of the hospital and returned to school, there was that look again. Not on the faces of my peers, that was a different look. But every teacher, even ones I did not know, looked at me with this 'poor thing' expression. And the kids, well, they literally walked around me, as though they could catch what I had. Rumors had spread of me being a drug addict, an alcoholic, having a sexually transmitted disease, and more. Nobody really knew what it was that I had. But they knew they did not want anything to do with it or with me.

Even my friends stopped texting, stopped inviting me to hang out with them. They just, well, stopped. The boys were just as bad. They did not seem to see me anymore and went out of their way to pretend I was not standing directly in front of them. I only went to school for a half-day a couple of times per week, and then not at all, as I preferred to work from home.

I had no energy and slept twelve to fourteen hours per day, and when I was not sleeping, I was just lying there. I was not depressed or anything. I just had no energy to do anything. I also had weird mood swings and got very angry, getting set off by the smallest thing. The only person I felt like being around was Peter, probably because his life was as out of control as mine was."

Bea trailed off and took a big and sudden intake of breath, sighed, and then stopped talking.

During the time since I had met Bea, this seemed to be her way, which I found very interesting. It was like she was locked up like Fort Knox until someone put in the right combination or found the right key, and then she opened up, and this whole amazing personality flooded out. And as suddenly as this happened, it would just stop again, and she would resume being locked up until the next time. I loved both sides of her personality and found them both charming, heart-warming, and desirable. The energy we created while we were together was just amazing. When she touched me, I felt like I was receiving an electric shock of the best kind.

The coming of spring meant it was time to apply to colleges and start planning the next step in our lives. Even though things were so different now, there was a part of me that could not help applying to Stanford, as I'd always planned. Instead of applying elsewhere, I kept it to Stanford and Skidmore, the college where Brandon taught and where Jeremy went.

Bea and I were planning a hike later today, and I was hoping to discuss her plans with her. I wanted to wait for her to bring up the subject, but I thought she might need a little push.

Since her brief hospital stay before Christmas, she had slowly been getting stronger. She really missed jogging but was told that it could cause some serious side effects, including ruptured blood vessels in her esophagus. This had something to do with the blood vessels in her liver not having any healthy tissue and wrapping around the esophagus. The strain of cardio activity could cause a rupture, which could lead to serious complications.

Hiking had become her new fix, as she was obsessive about keeping fit, especially since her prednisone medication caused her to have a ferocious appetite, which was hard to control.

I drove up the familiar driveway of Bea's home to see her waiting for me as usual on the porch swing. Her face lit up when she saw me smiling at her, and she skipped down the steps in her sneakers. She opened the passenger door and hopped in.

"Hi," she said with a grin. She leaned over and kissed me.

"Hey," I said back. "You seem happy today."

"I am happy today. Do you want to know why?" she said playfully.

"Why," I said, looking behind me as I turned the car around.

"Because I get to see my boyfriend and go hiking with him, annnndddd ... I made my famous turkey sandwiches for us to have a picnic."

"I do love your turkey sandwiches. Did you put—"

"Extra cranberry sauce, yes, I did." She kissed me again, this time on the cheek.

It was not every day Bea had this much energy, and it was so nice to see her this cheerful. Maybe today would be a good day to bring up college and see where her head was.

We drove to the Geyser Creek Trail, which had several waterfalls that were amazing to watch and listen to. The sound of the sheer volume of water cascading down the side of the cliff was almost indescribable. The water looked like a wall of blue satin threaded with silver, and we watched it tumble down, pounding the rocks in a thunderous roar.

"Amazing, isn't it?" Bea said with a huge grin.

"Sure is," I replied while smiling at her.

"So, what do you want to talk about?"

"How did you know?" I was truly shocked. Bea had this way of knowing what people were thinking and feeling. She was keenly aware of everyone around her, along with their emotional needs.

"I have my ways." She gave my arm a gentle push.

"Well, I wanted to talk to you about what you see happening in the fall."

Bea looked at me, her blue eyes blinding me with their brilliance. "I want you to do what feels right. I love you, Joel. I want you to go after your dreams, wherever they take you. My place, for now, is here. I was thinking of taking a year off school, spending lots of time with Peter, and maybe doing some volunteer work."

"What about school? You are an honor student. Weren't you talking to your mom about possibly going into gerontology? What about that?"

"I don't think school is the thing for me right now. Maybe never. I do not expect you to understand, but for me, things are not the same as they used to be. I want to live my life now, on my terms, and not waste any time." Bea looked down at her feet. "I can't explain it any better than that."

I stepped closer to Bea, feeling so in love with her that I could melt. Our eyes locked together, and I cupped her small face in my hands. "Bea, I love you. I will not ever pretend that I know how you feel, and I don't know what the future holds. But I can promise you this—I'm always going to be here for you."

When I kissed her, it was as though every emotion I had ever felt came crashing down on me. I felt dizzy, drunk, overwhelmed with desire for her. I wanted to take her in my arms and hold her tight and protect her with my last breath. We clung to one another, our bodies damp from the spray of the water, our hearts beating quickly and pounding loudly against each other's chests.

Over the coming weeks, I spent a lot of time working on my college entrance essays. I usually loved writing essays, but I just could not seem to concentrate on anything else but Bea these days. I wanted to spend all my time with her. As much as I liked to remain optimistic, there was always a feeling in the back of my mind like we had a time limit. The future that I had imagined for us had once seemed so exciting, but now it felt full of the unknown and under unavoidable restraints.

Ideas were forming in my mind, and I found myself deep in thought as I wrote in my journal. It felt good to have some extra time whenever Bea was busy taking care of Peter or going to follow-up appointments with her doctors. As much as I loved spending time with her, it was hard on my mental strength. I often found by the end of the day, I was exhausted and would pass out in my clothes with the lights on. It was not from physical strain, since Bea did not have much energy herself, but the emotional strain I felt every day while dealing with her illness was draining.

I loved her, and I desperately wanted her to get everything she desired out of her life, but I did not know how to make that happen for her. She could not travel to many countries because of foreign bacteria in the water and food. She could not even go in the ocean without a wetsuit and water shoes because if she had even one small cut, she could be susceptible to germs that were lethal to her condition.

I spent much of my days trying to work through all the medical terms and restrictions while always trying to find a way to make her as happy as I could. I had taken her to look at dresses a couple of times for graduation. Bea was not much of a girly girl, but she did get a cute smile on her face when she touched some of the silky gowns or tried on some shoes she liked. We had decided that going to prom was not something either of us wanted to do. Neither of us enjoyed dancing, and even though I had made a few friends here and there, I had pretty much kept to myself when I was not with Bea or her family. Anna was excited to go and had been asked by Eric from her music class. They had been texting non-stop for months. She claimed they were just good friends, but I was not too sure about that. He seemed like a cool guy, from what I knew of him, and I was excited for her.

With the warmer weather and all the fresh starts of spring I had never experienced before, these last few months of our high school career seemed precious. I think it was natural to feel like something was ending, but in fact, this was only the beginning. Sitting at my desk just weeks after I had sent my application to Stanford, I realized what an idiot I was.

There was nothing for me back in California. My future, and all the amazing people meant to be in it, was here now. Plans can change, and so can dreams. I had always dreamed of Stanford, but I now understood that it had not been my dream for some time now. My dream was Bea. My home was wherever she was, and she was my future.

I sat for several minutes, soaking this in before I reached for my laptop and started writing. I wrote for what must have been hours, but truthfully, I lost track. In the end, the words I had composed were honest and to the point in only two pages.

I reread it twice before sending it to the printer in the office. I got up and quickly looked in the mirror to make sure I looked alright, and I went to get the pages I had just written, grabbing my house keys on the way.

When I knocked on the Canning's front door, I knew Bea was with Peter, and Jeremy was at school. The person I was looking for was the one who answered.

"Joel," Brandon said when he saw me. "Bea and Jeremy aren't here right now, son."

"I know," I said. I clutched my paper tightly. "I wanted to see you."

"Oh? How can I help you?" Bea's father opened the door for me to go inside.

"I wrote something that I need you to read."

"Is it for school or college application?"

"Neither."

"I don't understand."

"I think you will understand better after reading it."

Brandon and I walked to his office, and he shut the door before having a seat behind his ornate wooden desk. I sat in the leather chair across from him and extended the folded papers in my hand, warm from my touch. Brandon seemed to hesitate for only a second before taking the papers, stealing a glance at me while he did.

He put his reading glasses on and started to consume the words I had so carefully chosen just for him. There was a long silence, and he seemed to read it slowly and cautiously. Those five minutes seemed like an eternity before he finished. My heart was pounding so hard I thought it might jump out of my chest.

"So, . . . ," Brandon said, carefully setting the paper down and taking his glasses off to stare at me. He seemed genuinely taken aback, although there was no outburst or expression of surprise. He did not yell, he did not cry, and he didn't say anything for several more moments. He just studied my face. I did not look away, keeping my eyes fixed on his with every bit of determination I had within me.

"You would like to marry my daughter," Brandon said, finally.

"Yes, sir, I would."

"Why?"

"For the reasons you just read."

"Joel, I know that you love my daughter, but you need to understand that she will never get better. You have your whole life ahead of you to live in perfect health and do anything you please. And you want to spend your days going to doctor's appointments and living with boundaries that will never go away before you've even gotten out of high school?"

"Sir, if you need to ask me this, then you don't understand my feelings for her. There is no future for me without her. There is not a day since I met her that I could live without her, and there never will be again. The world shifted on its axis the moment I laid eyes on her, and the pull of the universe began to rotate around her. It is not a choice. Bea is the woman I want to spend the rest of my life with."

Brandon stared at me with wide eyes. They were just as blue as Bea's, but with tired lines around them. I leaned forward, tense in my seat, waiting for his response, using every muscle in my body to focus the energy in the room so he would say yes. I waited, and we stared at each other for a few moments more of eternity before he opened his mouth again to speak.

"Then, you better treat her like it for the rest of your life."

I stood up, fighting the urge to burst into tears, to shout, to jump, to hug him even. "I promise you, starting today, I will spend every waking moment fighting for her smile. Starting today, this is forever."

Brandon nodded as he came around the desk to stand in front of me. He had tears in his eyes as he extended his hand to shake. I took it and pulled him into a hug. He put his arm around me and patted me stiffly on the back before pulling away and turning toward the window.

"When will you propose?" he asked, not looking at me.

"On her birthday, the moment she turns eighteen."

CHAPTER TEN

I t was warm and sunny again on the east coast. We were making summer plans, deciding on camping locations, figuring out our last-minute college details, and I was getting ready for something big. I had bought the ring.

I had picked it out last week. It was a white gold band that wrapped around the finger like a wave and held in place a perfect little diamond. I knew it was the one for Bea the moment I saw it, kind of like I had known she was the one for me. When you know, you know, right? It had cost most of my savings, but I did not mind in the slightest. I was ready to spend the rest of my life with her, be committed to her and everything she came with, and I wanted her to know.

I had been trying to figure out the way I would propose. I wanted to blow her away, but still, I knew something over the top was not her style. It had to be sweet, intimate, and simple.

Graduation had been an amazing day. We had all gotten dressed up, Jeremy and I in suits, Anna in a soft pink dress, and Bea in the most stunning silver slip dress. When I first saw her in that dress, I was not sure I could make it through the ceremony. I could not stop staring. It hugged her slender body perfectly and made her eyes look like ice. She had a little color from being in the sun, and she had gotten her hair styled in a loose bun with strands of curls framing her lovely face. I could not believe I was soon to be the luckiest guy alive. This was going to be my future wife.

We all sat together, Jeremy sneaking into the graduating student seating, and our parents sitting together a few seats behind us. We all went up and received our diplomas, grinning back at the others when we were on stage. When Bea went up, you could hear the room cheering a little extra for her, the teachers included. She had not had an easy high school journey, that much I knew. I think many people had wondered if she would make it to this day.

She looked beautiful on that stage, confident yet gentle at the same time. God, I loved her. When she came down, I was waiting for her with a big hug, and she whispered in my ear, "I did it!" I gave her a kiss on her forehead and said back, "You did it."

We all went down to the Saratoga Lake Marina to celebrate. Our moms had surprised us and planned a picnic with homemade burgers, potato salad, and my dad's famous homemade fries. We ate and laughed and chatted, taking in the excitement from the fact that we were all done with high school! I loved seeing my parents get along so well with Bea's. I couldn't wait until we were all family!

July fourth was fast approaching, which happened to be the day I had chosen to propose. It was Bea's eighteenth birthday, and it would be a day to remember forever. I had finally come up with what I imagined was the perfect proposal for my girl. Next was to get permission from Peter. I knew I needed to ask Peter, as Bea held his friendship so close to her heart. Bea was spending a lot of time at his home, volunteering to help some of the other residents with exercise and take them for walks around the pond. She was so good with them, and they seemed genuinely to love her.

Perhaps I'm biased, but honestly, who wouldn't love her. I would be going over to Peter's once she texted me that she was on her way home. After a quick visit with him to share my news, Bea and I were planning to go out for sushi with Anna, her new boyfriend Eric, Jeremy, and his latest lady friend Mia.

Bea: *Had a great day with everyone here. It's so amazing helping to put a smile on their faces. Peter has a new joke he's dying to share with you! Heading home for a quick shower. Can hardly wait to see you!! Xo*

Joel: *I am loving you so much right now. Xo*

That was my cue! I left the house and drove in anticipation until I reached the retirement home. I found Peter enjoying a cup of tea in his room. He was spread out in his easy chair with the rich sounds of Debussy playing in the background. Since meeting Peter and Tess, my appreciation for classical music had really grown. He had taught me how to distinguish between some of the greatest composers like Mozart, Beethoven, Rachmaninoff, Bach, and Debussy, who is my favorite.

"Hi, Peter! May I come in for a quick visit?" I said, knocking on the open door.

"Hello, Joel! You just missed Bea." He was smiling broadly.

"Did you have a good visit?"

"Bea is always a breath of fresh air!" He set down his cup of tea and folded his wrinkled hands in his lap.

"Hear any good jokes lately?" I said, remembering Bea's text.

Peter quickly got into a long story about three nuns sitting on a park bench. Before long, he was laughing so hard, he spilled his tea. I quickly crossed the room to help him. Once I got him sorted out, I sat back down. Peter must have sensed my apprehension.

"Is everything okay?" he asked.

"Everything is amazing. I wanted to run something by you, though. Is this a good time?"

"Now is just as good a time as any," Peter said. "What's on your mind?"

"I'm going to propose to Bea and would really like your blessing, Peter."

Peter regarded me intently and slowly opened his mouth. "What was that?"

Okay, I guess he had not heard me. I took another stabilizing breath and started again. "I would like to ask Bea to marry me and would like your blessing, Peter."

Again, he looked at me, this time cocking one eyebrow. "Say again?"

I stood up and took a step closer to Peter. Maybe it was time he got a hearing aid. Peter reached out and pulled me closer, laughing uproariously. "I'm just pulling your leg, Joel. Reach down here and give me a hug."

I smiled with relief. "Always ready to play a prank, aren't you? Well, what do you think? Is that your way of saying you approve?"

"Of course. I am so happy for both of you. If she says yes, that is." He smiled mischievously in my direction, checking to see if he had yet again gotten a rise out of me.

Peter spent the next half hour down memory lane, letting me in on how he had proposed to Tess. "Don't ever let her know I told you this now, young lad, but I dropped a diamond ring in Tess's glass of beer, and she nearly choked on the damned thing!" We roared with laughter, tears flowing freely from Peter's eyes.

I stayed with Peter for a little while before going to meet Bea and the others for sushi. When I picked up Bea and Jeremy, Jeremy jumped down the steps and jogged toward the car. Bea delicately walked at a slow pace, as if careful, reminding me how fragile she was.

"Hey, man!" Jeremy said as he hopped into the backseat. "No BMW today, eh?"

"Not today, Jer," I said.

"Darn," Jeremy said absentmindedly as he looked for his seatbelt. Bea had gotten in next to me, smiling as she sat down gently.

"Hi," I said, reaching over to kiss her.

"Hey," she said back, parting her lips when my own touched them.

"Okay, get a room, eh?" Jeremy said, laughing. "By the way, where's Anna?"

"She's going with Eric, and they'll meet us there."

The sushi place in town was beautifully decorated, much like the place Bea and I had gone on our first date. This place was much smaller and more modest, but we had been here a few times, and the California rolls were the best.

We picked up Mia on the way, and Anna and Eric were there when we arrived. We were seated right away at the big table by the window. Our order came on a boat platter to our happiness as it was beautiful and colorful and tasted amazing. We all chatted for a while as we started to dig in, and I piped up when the moment was right.

"Hey, guys, there's something I gotta tell ya," I said after swallowing a salmon roll.

Bea looked at me intently, and everyone's attention was on me.

"What's up?" Jeremy asked without stopping his consumption of food.

"Well, as you guys know, I've always wanted to go to Stanford, and I actually got in." I felt Bea's body tense next to me. I reached for her hand and squeezed it.

"It would have been a dream come true to study there like my parents did. But I realize now that there is a new dream in my mind, one that I can't shake." Everyone waited. "It's being here, with all of you. So, I'm excited to announce that I have accepted my offer to attend Skidmore University."

"Yeah, man!" Jeremy said, clapping. Anna clapped too and gave out a woohoo! Eric and Mia followed their leads, and I looked at Bea. She did not say anything, but she clapped with a look of relief and contentment that made everything I'd been so nervous about seem alright. I leaned over and kissed her on the cheek, and she held onto me so gently, and I noticed tears in her ocean blue eyes.

Bea: *I love you I love you I love you.*

The following morning could not have been more beautiful. The sky was as brilliant a blue as the shimmering swimming pool in our backyard. The birds were chirping loudly, and everything I looked at seemed crystal clear. The excitement flowed through my veins, and I did not know what to do with myself until tonight. I was so excited and nervous that my heart was ready to beat right out of my chest. So far, only Brandon and Peter knew of my plan to propose to Bea tonight at midnight, the moment she turned eighteen.

I spent the morning and afternoon in the backyard, helping with the yard work and vacuuming the pool. My mom and dad loved entertaining, and they were hosting a July fourth celebration and wanted to make things perfect. Anna was elbow deep in dirt as she weeded the garden alongside mom and dad, who were stringing stylish Japanese lanterns around the large deck. It was beautiful with three tiers and built-in benches, a rectangular sail shade, a large stunning pergola designed out of bamboo, and patio furniture covered in Japanese designs. I caught my mom eyeing me with interest.

"Joel, you haven't stopped smiling all day!" she said. "You and Bea must be really enjoying the start of summer."

"Yep!" I was dying to tell my folks and Anna, but I wanted Bea and me to announce our engagement tomorrow night, so I just had to keep this to myself. It was not easy. Thank God Anna was too wrapped up in her phone to notice since I could never keep anything from her.

"Anna, are you going to invite your new boyfriend to the Fourth of July party tomorrow night?" Dad teased her. Anna looked up and gave Dad a look that would serve to quiet him as she shook her fist in the air. My mom and I laughed.

"Let me know what else I can do to help later. I am just going to take a quick break and do a little writing. Cool?" I forced myself to look serious, making sure to frown as I walked past them as they were taking a break and enjoying a glass of white wine under the pergola.

"Sure," they replied in unison and laughed.

Once in my room, I could smile again, and as I passed my bureau mirror and jumped onto my bed, journal in hand, I caught the goofy smile in the reflection. Oh, man. What if she says we are too young? What if she straight up says no? What if . . . ?

I uncapped my favorite pen and began writing in the journal Bea had given me as a gift for Christmas. Thinking back on those first few days after learning about her condition tore at my heart. Every day I remembered the reality of the situation. I learned more of the things that Bea had to watch out for, like alcohol, as even a sip could kill her. She could not be directly in the sun. She had severe osteoporosis, and as a result, she was not encouraged to play sports, participate in any cardio exercise, go skydiving, or do any winter sports, including tobogganing.

She had to be careful lifting and should not even do a crunch due to the fragility of her bones. This wasn't even including the no-travel-at-any-cost-right-now rule, the foods she should stay away from, and the constant worry of acquiring a secondary illness as a result of the slew of medications she was on. Every morning and evening, she had a cocktail of meds she popped like candy. She kept them in a large red checked bag with a moose on the front, her favorite animal. No matter how incredible the conversation that was going on, everyone sobered up the moment the zipper of that bag was heard.

July 3

I am going to be a husband. I never thought this would be happening so fast. I'd always imagined meeting my future wife at Stanford, in one of my literature classes, a pair of glasses on the end of her nose, which was buried deep in a copy of The Sun Also Rises or Tender is the Night. I know that most guys my age are just getting started on the party scene, adding up the kegs they've drunk and putting as many notches on their belt as they can. For me, those days will never come, and I don't care in the slightest. Bea has stolen my heart, and my life is hers. I will treasure her until my last breath, someday when we are both old and gray, just like Peter and Tess. Please say yes, my angel, and make me the happiest man alive.

I must have fallen asleep because when I woke up, the light had dimmed outside my window and the air that flowed through had a slight nip. My stomach suddenly lurched as I grabbed my phone and read the time—8:22 p.m. Almost three more hours. I smiled once again and walked into my bathroom, turned on the hot water, and got ready to take a shower. I put on Bea's favorite jeans and shirt and splashed on my favorite cologne, Castle Forbes. I ran down to the family room where my sister and Eric sat devouring pizza.

"Hey, guys!" I said, coming into the room. "Where's Mom and Dad?"

"They went to the butcher to grab some steaks. Want a piece of pizza?"

"No thanks, I'm not that hungry." My stomach felt like there was a symphony of butterflies in it. I was not nervous as much as I was completely and utterly excited.

I had everything planned out. At 11:50, I was going to hoist myself through Bea's window with a rose. She always went to bed at 11:00 and either read, listened to music or podcasts, or watched Netflix in bed until she fell asleep. I joined Anna and Eric on the couch where they were watching a rerun of the Big Bang Theory.

"You going out with Bea tonight as an early birthday celebration?" Anna asked.

"No, she's just going to hang in tonight." I realized I both looked and smelled like I was going out. In an effort to distract from getting any more attention, I lied. "She wasn't feeling great and changed plans at the last minute. I guess you guys are stuck with me."

Both Anna and Eric groaned, and I chucked an oversized charcoal pillow at them. Anna added, "I hope she feels good for her birthday tomorrow. That would suck if she couldn't enjoy it!"

I texted Bea: *Dear almost birthday girl, I hope you had a nice night watching a movie with your mom. I can't wait to see you tomorrow morning for your birthday brunch. Tons of love and sweet dreams xo.*

The time finally came, and the house was quiet. Mom and Dad always go to bed early and wake up at the crack of dawn. Eric had to pick up his little sister at work, and Anna was up in her room, doing Anna things. I ran upstairs, pulled open my bedside drawer, and pocketed the midnight blue velvet box that held Bea's ring.

CHAPTER ELEVEN

t was 11:30 p.m. on July third, just a half-hour before Bea's birthday and my proposal. I snuck over to her house, being careful that nobody was looking out the window or sitting on the porch swing. It felt surreal, like I was in a dream. It was crazy that this was happening, that I was actually doing this. In my heart, I knew she would say yes, but I still felt like I was going to throw up.

I crossed the manicured front lawn and neared Bea's bedroom window, gathering my courage. I saw the faint glow of her phone and could see her lying in bed. I stopped suddenly, frozen with excitement.

I pulled my phone out of my pocket and texted: *Look out your window.*

It was 11:58 p.m., so I had to wait two minutes before pressing send. I saw her look up at the window although she could not see me, and she got out of bed.

I held the bouquet of roses in my shaking hands and waited. Moments later, Bea slid open the window, "Hey! What are you doing here?"

"I wanted to be the first to wish you a happy birthday." I handed her the roses, and she smelled them.

"They're so beautiful. White roses, my favorite! I can't believe you." She leaned on the windowsill as I stood just outside, looking at my future wife.

"There is something else." I pulled myself up into the window frame and crawled through as she stepped back to let me in. Once inside, I took a deep breath, looked at her one last time before everything was different, and I went down on one knee.

I heard Bea take a quick intake of breath as she brought both hands up to her face, covering her mouth. "Bea," I said seriously. "My life is more vibrant when I see you smile, and your smile has given my life a new purpose. I never want this to end. Will you marry me?"

Bea blinked, tears springing out of her eyes as I opened the box with the sparkling ring. I held my breath.

She softly answered, "Yes." Bea began to cry quietly. "I can't believe this is happening."

I took the ring out and placed it on her finger as tears of my own slowly came down my cheek. I took Bea's face in my hands and leaned down to kiss her. Our emotions were soaring as our kiss deepened. I stopped long enough to pick her up, and I placed her on her bed, and we shared our love in the most romantic moment of my entire life. Nothing could have prepared me for the depth of feeling that threatened to devour me. This girl, this beautiful girl was everything—the sun, moon, stars, ocean, the entire universe. We fell asleep, both exhausted from the raw emotions that invaded us, mind, body, and soul. I awoke at 2:30 a.m., quietly covered Bea with her blanket, and slipped out the window. I hoped the roses would make it until morning.

I woke up flying so high all I wanted to do was run around yelling she said yes!!! I was so beside myself. Last night was the most incredible night of my life. I did not even know it was possible to be that amazing. Bea had said yes. Yes! YES!!

My life is on a crash collision course with heaven on earth. Having Bea in my life is one thing, but having her as my wife, the one person I would get to spend my days and nights with, share myself with. I'd get to breathe the same air, watch her sleep, wake up and see her face, go to bed with her in my arms. Nothing could bring me down today. Today is perfect in every way. The fact that it's the Fourth of July only serves to intensify the excitement of the day.

Joel: *Good morning future Mrs. Peterson. I feel like a new man today. Thank you for loving me even a tiny bit as much as I love you. See you soon!! Xoxo*

I knew I just had to put things out of my mind until I could tell the world tonight, so I thought about our incredible night instead to get me through until the afternoon and festivities at my place. Her lips had been so soft, and when I kissed her neck, she squirmed in my arms, her body pressed tightly against mine.

Before meeting Bea, it had been a long time since I had been physically involved with a girl, and we'd only kissed and explored a bit. But never had I been so emotionally involved at the same time. My body and soul felt like they belonged fused with hers.

I sent Bea another text: *I will love you forever.*

Bea: *I am scared. But I'm so happy that it's you I am scared with. You are the one I want to roll over into in the middle of the night and wake up to every day for the rest of my life. You're the one I want to go on exciting adventures with. Jump out of planes with, jump off cliffs with, swim to the bottom of the ocean with. You're the one I want to go on exhilarating adventures with, such as hikes in the woods, jaunts on a fast boat or ATV, or walk up a mountainside with. You're the one I want to stay in with for the night and build a cute fort where we can watch movies and hold hands. You're the one I want to make happy for the rest of my life. You're the one I want to love and to hold when times get tough. You're the one who I want to be there if the world comes crashing down. You're the one I want to taste new foods with. You're the one I want to kiss for hours on end. All my good days and my bad days, you're the one I want to spend them with. It's you. You're him. You are the one.*

Bea: *Speechless? Good! You're the one.*

Joel: *I was in the shower. Wow. I read this message, and my mind is going berserk! All I keep picturing is all the things we will get to do together for the first time and for the hundredth time. I dreamt of the day I would meet the woman of my dreams, the one who wanted to do all the things I want to do and introduce to me things I have never thought of doing, and I no longer have to dream because you have made my dreams a reality, and I cannot wait to thank you and be so grateful to you for the rest of my life. Xo*

Joel: *Thank you and keep telling me I'm the one. I love hearing those words. It fills me with such joy.*

Bea: *You're the one.*

Bea: *You're the one.*

Bea: *You're the one.*

Everything looked perfect in the back yard for the barbecue. The Cannings had arrived first, and I had to refrain from grabbing Bea when I saw her. I caught her sneaking glimpses of me while I rounded up drinks for Anna, Eric, Jeremy, and Mia. I made sure there was plenty of pop and juice for Bea and me. I could not help noticing how she eyed the glasses of wine and champagne like they were poison.

Peter and Tess arrived late, but I think Peter enjoyed the extra attention he received as Bea and our moms rushed to help them through the back fence and make sure they were okay. Peter caught my eye and raised his eyebrows in question. In response, I nodded with a huge grin on my face. He returned my smile with one of his own as he reached for Tess's arm to steady himself. He was still not able to get around too well, but we had found out a few weeks before that Peter had been cleared to return home. They did not seem too rushed to get there, and Bea and I thought perhaps they had begun liking the retirement home. It sure was convenient, with the nurses and competent staff always on call and ready to help in any manner necessary.

I sat next to Bea, holding her hand tightly in mine. Bea agreed to leave her ring in her pocket and was planning on slipping it on after we told everyone. I could not wait. We were both so excited to share our news. I kept checking the time on my phone. I squeezed her hand and leaned down to whisper, "I love you." Who knew that three tiny words could mean so much. I wanted to stand up and shout it to the world and did not think that waiting long for our wedding was even possible. I wanted to marry Bea now, today if I could.

"This is good beer," Jeremy said, gulping the craft beer my dad had picked out. "I think I'm going to have to get this beer from now on. The guys would love it. Maybe they have kegs?"

Anna rolled her eyes. "No, Jer, they do not have kegs. It's craft beer from a local artisanal brewery."

"I don't know what that means, but it would be good to party with this stuff." He nudged Mia, who nearly spilled her glass of red wine. She looked at him irritably. Jeremy did not notice.

"We're going to have some great times this summer, buddy," I said, smiling at Jeremy.

"Hell, yeah, we are! Camping next weekend, right? It's supposed to be even hotter than last week."

"Sounds good," I said, giving Bea's hand a squeeze. Brandon neared our group, looking a little uncertain.

"Joel, would you mind showing me where I can get more ice?" He said this in a deep, serious voice that led me to believe he meant something else.

"Yeah, sure," I said. "Be right back." I kissed Bea on the cheek and followed Brandon into the house. He seemed to know exactly where he was going and pretty much led me to the kitchen. I went over to the freezer and pulled out one of the bags of ice we'd bought earlier in the day.

"What did she say?" Brandon asked seriously.

"She said yes," I replied.

He was silent for a moment, nodding as he leaned against the counter and eyed the glass of vodka soda in his hands.

"There's something you need to know, Joel," he said. "There will come a day in Bea's life where she will need a liver transplant. It's unclear when that day will come, but when it does, she will need it within forty-eight hours or face imminent death."

My heart stopped at those last two words, all the feeling leaving my legs as if I were frozen in place.

"I know that you love Bea, and I support your union. But you need to know just what you're dealing with if you're going to be there until the end. I don't mean to worry you on your happy day, but I just need to know that you realize the severity of her condition."

I swallowed and let out the air I had been holding in since he started speaking. "Like they say, in sickness and in health. I will be there for her when that day comes. I'll be there every day until then, and every day after."

Brandon looked like he might cry. He just stood there, nodding until he could not hold it in anymore. "Thank you, Joel." He shut his eyes, and tears streamed down his face. "All I've ever wanted for her was to find someone like you."

Tears started in my own eyes, and I went over and put a hand on his shoulder. We stood there for a few minutes, feeling our emotions fully. "Okay," Brandon said, collecting himself. "Come on, the ice will melt."

It was time for dinner, as the steaks and all the trimmings were placed around the huge outdoor dining table. My dad helped Tess and Peter to the seats of honor, and everyone else slowly made their way to their seats. It was my father's custom to say a blessing before eating when we had company, and when he finished, I stood up.

"I just wanted to thank you all as well for coming tonight to celebrate with us this year!" I looked to my right and extended my hand to Bea, pulling her up gently. "This year, I have to say, will be my favorite July fourth celebration. Not only is it Bea's eighteenth birthday, but it's also . . . ," I paused from the lump of emotion that had suddenly formed in my throat. "It's also the day I get to announce to all of my favorite people that Bea and I are engaged!"

I looked at Bea and took the ring that she had been holding in her closed hand, and I placed the ring back where it belonged. Everyone cheered and clinked their glasses together. My parents looked so happy. My mom even started crying. Brandon and Ria kissed in celebration, and Peter gave us one of his famous winks.

After the tears had been shed, and congratulations made, Peter stood up shakily.

"I would like to say something to everyone. You have all been such a blessing to Tess and me. I have always wondered what I might have done in another lifetime to deserve this woman seated beside me, but also to have been given a second girl, who is as much my daughter as any daughter could ever be. Bea, Joel, you are the most stunning couple I have ever had the pleasure of knowing, and the two of you are the most important people in our lives. That is why Tess has decided to move in with me at the retirement home, and we will be selling our properties, all except one. We would like to give our country cottage and its furnishings to Bea and Joel as a wedding present. I hope you'll accept it." He tossed the keys in our direction, and I caught them, so surprised that I felt like I was in a dream.

"Oh my gosh, Peter, Tess, I don't know how to thank you," Bea said through her tears.

"Just promise me you'll have lots of babies and share laughter and love for years to come!" Peter replied, his voice shaky with emotion. One look around the table revealed there wasn't one dry eye. I was grateful when Jeremy spoke up, and in his usual hurried manner around food, he announced, "We love you guys, congratulations. Now let's eat!"

Over the next month, Bea and I spent most of our days packing, planning, and loving every moment we got to spend with one another. I noticed Bea's energy draining away at an alarming rate. She continued meeting her weekly blood withdrawals and had several appointments with various doctors. We were almost ready to move into our new home, with all of Tess and Peter's lovely furniture in place, and Bea's mom had almost finished cleaning up the gardens. I was waiting for Bea at my parents' place as she had some sort of surprise for me. She came to the door holding a bandana in one hand, wearing a silky gold sundress.

"You are going to love this, Joel. Just relax and be patient."

I laughed. "Okay, what do you have planned, Mrs. Peterson?"

She giggled and tied the bandana around my eyes. "Don't worry about it, Mr. Peterson."

After a short drive, Bea stopped the car. I knew immediately where we were.

"No peeking," Bea warned. She led me out of the vehicle and locked arms with me as we walked down the pebbly path. I heard a squeaky door open as she helped me to step inside.

"Okay, you can look now!"

I took off the eye covering to find that I was standing in Tess and Peter's cottage, our new home, with small twinkling lights hanging everywhere, fresh flowers from our garden on all the surfaces, and a salmon dinner sitting on a candlelit table.

"Surprise!" she said excitedly.

"You did all this?" I said, looking around.

"Tess helped me. Do you like it?"

"I love it. You're amazing."

She went over to the dining table and motioned for me to come and sit. She pulled out a chair, and I sat down. She kissed me on the cheek and then sat in the chair across from me. The salmon was still warm, and she had made Brussels sprouts and cooked carrots. There was a bottle of non-alcoholic wine on the table, and we had two stemmed wine glasses.

"I wanted our first dinner in our new home to be special," she said, tucking a strand of blonde hair behind her ear.

"It's perfect," I said.

"Bon appetit!" She grabbed her fork and knife.

I did the same and took a bite of the delicious-looking salmon. It melted in my mouth.

"I didn't know you could cook something like this."

"My dad has taught me many recipes over the last couple of weeks." She looked a little embarrassed. "So, I can be a good wife and make us dinner. Sorry if it's a little cold."

I melted even more than the salmon when I heard this. "That's actually so cute. I'll have to learn some recipes to make for you as well, and I love cold salmon just as much!"

We had an amazing dinner with great conversation and sat there drinking the fake wine and chatting until it started getting dark out. "Come on," Bea said, grinning. She got up and went to the door.

"Where are we going now?" I asked, following her outside.

She gently jogged down to the small pond in the expansive yard. I'd learned from Tess that this cottage was nestled in the middle of fifty acres of trees imported from all around the world. It had been in the family for generations. There was one main cottage decorated in beautiful farmhouse décor and two smaller cottages located down by a running stream near the back of the property. It was a heavenly home to many animals, including deer, coyotes, herons, and other furry creatures.

The pond was surrounded by lilies and daisies, and there was a swan family who lived there. Bea reached the water's edge and began taking off her dress. She undid the zipper and lifted it up over her head, revealing her delicate, sun-kissed body and floral underwear.

She looked at me expectantly. "Your turn."

"We're going swimming?" I asked.

My question was answered when she ran into the pond, splashing as she went. I stripped down to just my briefs and followed her in. I would have followed her anywhere.

I reached her in the center of the pond and put my arms around her back and under her legs. We floated like that, for I do not know how long, just staring at each other and smiling. It was twilight, and the fireflies came out just like on our first date. This place was magical and had so much love within the property. You could feel it when you drove up to the cottage, when you were inside, or even sitting in the gardens. I could not believe it was ours to start a life here, raise a family, and make it where our story takes place.

I felt Bea shiver in my arms, and I was brought back to the present moment. "Are you cold?" I asked. She nodded. "Let's go inside."

We went inside and pulled out some fluffy pink towels from the linen closet. I wrapped Bea in one and wrapped another around myself. After we were dry, I took our wet underwear and tossed them in the dryer. When I came back, Bea had gotten into bed in our new room. I had never spent much time in bed with her and couldn't believe we were going to be sleeping in this bed together every night now. I went to get in with her and realized she was fast asleep. I carefully slipped under the covers and rested my head next to hers on the pillow. I let sleep cave in on me and let my dreams unravel.

CHAPTER TWELVE

I woke up the next morning and heard the most extraordinary sounds coming from outside. Birds had congregated outside the window, some chirping, tweeting, and others in full song. The chirps came in bursts, bringing a small smile to my lips. They were calling to one another, the songs coming from different trees that lined the property. I wondered what they were saying. I had noticed a bird book, well used, on the bureau a few days ago. Now I understood why.

It was no wonder Peter spoke so fondly and often of this beloved cottage. I had learned it was a favorite spot for many of Tess and Peter's friends as they gathered there for special holidays throughout the year. The furnishings and tasteful décor were gorgeous and cozy. It was the kind of place you never wanted to leave, and the world outside seemed very far away. It was an oasis!

I looked beside me and watched Bea sleeping soundly, her hair covering most of her face, one arm disappearing under her pillow, and the other arm holding the blanket up to her chin. She looked so fragile that it scared me for a moment. I remembered the words Brandon had spoken a month ago as we stood in my kitchen. He had looked so vulnerable, and the worry that etched his face deepened into a frown of anxiety. How long would she be able to keep her liver functioning at less than 7 percent? What would happen when she needed a transplant? Had he really been right about the forty-eight hours or imminent death? I had to remind myself that she was a fighter. I knew she had what it took to beat this illness.

I rose without making a sound, hoping to let Bea sleep in as long as possible. I made coffee and then walked barefoot to the big bay window with the sheer white curtains and noticed the kaleidoscope of colors dancing in view in every direction. No wonder Peter loved this place so much. It was the most beautiful place I had ever been to. I had seen some beautiful places growing up in California, but it was the tranquility of the setting here that was amazing. The more I looked around, the more life I noticed bustling around the cottage.

Red squirrels, chipmunks, and black squirrels with bushy tails fought over fallen seeds from nearby trees. Ducks and geese frolicked in the water in each of the ponds located at the side and back of the property. Birds frequently crisscrossed in patterns across the morning sky. I imagined all the other wildlife that had made homes within the forest surrounding the cottage—deer, raccoons, rabbits, skunks, porcupines, snakes.

Part of me wanted to wake Bea so she would not miss anything. I had to keep reminding myself that this was now our home. I looked down toward the pond where we had gone swimming the night before and imagined our kids splashing in the water. I wondered if Bea even wanted to have children. I let my mind wander and made a mental note to ask her about it. I also wondered if she wanted a pet, and if so, which kind. Did Bea know how much I loved dogs? What if she didn't and was more of a cat person? I hated cats. Well, hate is a strong word. Let's just say I'd never met a cat that was even the slightest bit friendly.

I heard a splash and saw a family of mallard ducks waddling down into the pond, their bright orange feet disappearing into the cool water. This must be why Peter was so fond of feeding the ducks, as it must have reminded him of home.

"Good morning!" I heard Bea's sweet voice and turned around.

"Well, sleeping beauty is awake! Come on over here. Wait until you see all the birds. It is crazy. I've never seen or heard so many varieties in one place. Did you sleep well?"

Bea crossed the few feet into my outstretched arms. Ah. Nothing else could feel this good.

Bea yawned and stretched both arms over her head. We both heard at the same time the sound of a car approaching. We looked at one another with surprise and a little unsure of what to do. We were not exactly ready for company. We did not have to worry, as we then heard the car disappear just as quickly.

We walked to the front door after agreeing that it sounded like Bea's mother's car. I opened the door and looked around outside, and I noticed a backpack. I reached down to pick it up when Bea recognized it.

"Oh my gosh, that's the one my mom and I were looking at online last week! Let's see what's inside!" Bea was very excited.

The backpack was a picnic pack filled with grapes, two small baguettes, a bottle of sparkling water, brie, a pint of raspberries, and Genoa salami, my favorite. There were two wine glasses, a blue-and-white checked picnic cover, cutlery for two, along with matching napkins.

"That was so sweet of my mom to bring this! Let's get changed and have a picnic out by the willow tree. C'mon!" Bea pulled me in and kissed my cheek, a gleeful expression on her face.

We settled ourselves in the perfect spot under a shady tree, and Bea poured some sparkling water in the two wine glasses.

"Are you having a nice time?" I asked Bea, noticing her relaxed demeanor. "I haven't seen you smile so much since the first day we met."

"That's because you haven't noticed all the times I'm smiling at you when you're not looking. How about you? You aren't having any second thoughts yet, are you?"

"Are you kidding me? You have made me the happiest guy that has ever lived. I cannot get over how fast all this happened and how empty my life had been before meeting you. I mean, seriously, if you had told me a year ago that I'd be engaged to the most beautiful, wonderful woman on this earth just fresh out of high school, I'd have died laughing. People are going to think we're crazy. You know, don't you?"

"Yep, and they would be right, wouldn't they? All I know is that crazy is perfect for us. I half expected to remain single for the rest of my life. I was not even interested in guys. I had Jeremy for company and Peter even though I know he's as old as the hills, but it really doesn't feel that way when we're together. We can talk for hours about anything. I remember playing him the latest

Justin Bieber album, and he grimaced all the way through, but then I put in Greta Van Fleet, and he loved it. Just like when we listen to his music, I could sit and listen to his favorite operas and composers all day. We even enjoy the same movies. That reminds me, he and I have a date tomorrow night to watch *The Notebook*, one of our favorites."

"Bea, let's play a game. How about we take turns asking each other things we wonder about, like, do you want to get a pet?"

"Oh, yes! I would love a dog. They are the best. We used to have a Munsterlander named Mandy. She only had one eye. She died a few years ago. What about you? Do you like dogs?"

"I sure do. Okay, now you ask me something."

"Which is your favorite, going out for pizza or sushi?"

"Uh, that's a hard one. I think I'm going to go with pizza." Bea threw a raspberry at my head.

"No! Well, we'll have to take turns picking restaurants then."

"My turn. Kids?" I looked at her hopefully.

"Yep! I'd like to have three girls. That way, the house will always be filled with warmth, flowers, and you'll always be taken care of."

Bea looked away as she said that with a thoughtful look on her face. I wondered what she was thinking. I knew she was afraid of her health situation, and I wanted so badly to take care of her and to alleviate some of her worry.

"Sounds nice, but they'll have to get in line behind you because you're the one I'm expecting is going to take care of me!"

We spent the entire morning and afternoon talking, laughing, and I was not surprised to realize I was falling more and more in love with her as the seconds passed. At one point, I'd run into the house to grab us some more water to drink, and on a whim, I brought along a small pad of paper, a pen, and an old glass mason jar that I found in the garage. I also grabbed a small spade.

We took turns writing down five dreams we each had on little pieces of paper, folding them, keeping them to ourselves, and then placing them in the jar. I dug a small hole next to a large rock near the tree that we'd fondly named George, and we agreed to dig up our little time capsule five years from today.

Having lost all sense of time, Bea and I headed back to the house. Time was sure a funny thing. One minute it was morning coffee, then a surprise picnic lunch, and before long, it was already time for dinner.

"I'm hungry. Do you enjoy having breakfast for dinner, Joel?"

"You read my mind, Mrs. Peterson."

A few hours later, after finishing a dinner of fried eggs, crisp bacon, and fresh sliced tomatoes from the garden, Bea and I sat at the kitchen table, each lost in our own happy thoughts. From the angle I was sitting, I would swear I could see a tinge of yellow in the corner of Bea's eye. I became worried but did not want to overreact or spoil the unbelievably romantic time we were having. Bea deserved to feel relaxed and carefree, even while her red-and-black checked medicine bag taunted us from its place on the corner of the counter.

By the end of the weekend, we had learned everything we could about one another. Bea had even thrown in a few shockers like her dream of swimming with the sharks and how she wanted to go skydiving, despite the warnings from her doctors. I also learned that more than anything, Bea wanted to climb Mount Everest one day. That really made me smile. I had seen the books on the shelf in their family room, and every book that had been written on Mount Everest was displayed. I had just assumed they were Brandon's or Jeremy's. I made a mental note to investigate tour companies that might offer trekking to the base camp or something along those lines.

Bea and I cleaned everything up, leaving our new home perfect for our moving in date next weekend. I dropped her off at her place, promising to swing by later to watch a movie with her and the family.

And just like that, our beautiful, perfect weekend came to a grinding halt and turned into hell, as Ria noticed the yellow tinge to Bea's eyes and her flushed appearance. Bea had spiked a fever. I learned that fevers were not to be taken lightly where Bea was concerned. Ria insisted on calling Dr. Cooper and arranged to meet him at the hospital that evening.

A few hours after I had returned home after dropping Bea off, she texted me to fill me in on the details, also letting me know that she was being admitted for observation and for tests. She assured me that this was routine and wished me goodnight, reminding me of how much she loved me. I grabbed my journal and thought warm thoughts of holding Bea in my heart until I could hold her in my arms once again.

CHAPTER THIRTEEN

I was about to go to bed a couple of hours later when I got a text from Ria saying that Bea had been moved to the ICU. I hurried back to the hospital, practically running up the stairs in my desperation to get to Bea. Out of breath and with fear stabbing at my chest, I neared the front desk where the nurses with serious expressions busily checked charts and spoke in soft whispers.

"Bea Canning?" I asked frantically, looking at the nurses, not caring if I interrupted. I felt a hand on my shoulder, and I spun around.

"Hi, honey." Ria smiled up at me warmly. "She's okay. They want her in ICU because she has developed an infection, and with her illness, she does not have an immune system. So, they are not letting us see her just now. We must wait until the fever breaks. It's just a precaution."

"Does she have her phone? Can I text her?" I asked, still frantic.

"Of course, dear, but maybe wait until morning. Brandon and I are about to head home since they expect Bea will sleep most of the night. Well, if you can call it sleep with all those machines humming and beeping and nurses coming in to check your vitals every two hours. I am sure by morning she will feel much better.

We are so thankful you have come into her life, Joel. You have a future of love and happiness together. I know it. So, go home and get some good sleep, free from worry. She'll be just fine, and you'll see her tomorrow."

I calmed down a bit at Ria's soothing tone and her reassuring words. I looked down the hall to where I knew the girl I loved was lying alone, with an illness we could not ignore, no matter how many perfect weekends we had. Turning to walk to the elevator with Ria, I suddenly thought of Jeremy and wondered why he was not here. I checked my phone and realized it had been turned off. There were six texts from Jeremy.

The most recent one read: *Joel, can you come get me, pls? I am at the Saratoga City Tavern, and I'm really drunk. Don't tell Bea.*

I quickly texted him back: *Be there in ten.*

I saw Jeremy through a window leaning against a bench, alone. He looked far from sober, except for the sobering expression he wore on his face. It was a look of deep despair, and I immediately felt worried. Now I had another Canning to be concerned for.

When he saw me pull up alongside the curb, he got up, wobbling until he was vertical. I wondered where Mia and the rest of his friends had gone. He walked over crookedly and, after a couple of attempts, figured out how to open the car door.

"Thanks for coming, man," he said, falling into the passenger seat.

"Where's Mia?" I asked, taking one last look around.

"We got into an argument, and I ended up telling her I just wanted to be alone," he said with a slight slur to his voice. "So, she left, man. I think everyone went to some party. I was not really in the mood."

"You seem to be in a mood for sure," I said and backed out of the parking lot.

"What is it with everyone always getting drunk and partying, anyway? It's so not cool," Jeremy went on.

"You're drunk, Jer."

"Bea's never had a drink in her life, and she is way more fun than those losers. Even after all she goes through. That is why you can't tell her about this, Joel. You can't."

"I can promise you I won't bring it up, but I won't lie to her if she asks," I said honestly.

"Ah, man. I just cannot believe this is happening again, and just when life is going right for her. It's so unfair."

After a few more similar comments, Jeremy joined my silence, and we drove to his house without another word. I was replaying those words. I just can't believe this is happening again. Those words really impacted me. I decided that moment that I would do whatever necessary to change Bea's situation in any way I could.

I stopped in front of Jeremy and Bea's house, and Jer looked at his sister's darkened bedroom window and then back at me. "Can I crash at your place? I just can't . . . you have no idea how many times . . . don't know what's gonna happen next . . . it's just too much." He put his head in his lap and covered it with his hands.

I put the car into drive and drove home. When we got there, I got out and went around to help Jeremy out of the car. Before opening his door, I took out my phone and sent a quick text to Ria, letting her know Jeremy was staying over. Then, I texted Bea.

Jeremy is staying at my place tonight. We will be at the hospital in the morning. Sleep well. I love you.

The night was sticky with a warm breeze, and the stars twinkled in the distance, promising a beautiful day tomorrow. I opened the passenger door, and Jeremy stayed where he was with his face in his lap.

"Come on, man, let's get you inside," I encouraged.

Jeremy shook his head. "I can't. Just leave me here."

"I'm not leaving you here, Jer," I said. "Come on. You can go right to sleep when we get inside."

Jeremy slowly got out of the vehicle, and I helped him up the driveway. I tried to be quiet when we got in, but Jeremy stumbled in and smacked his head on the door frame.

"Ouch, you alright?" I whispered, wincing at the loud bang.

"I can't feel anything right now," Jeremy said with a sigh. I led him to the couch in the living room, and he fell face-first into it. He groaned and tossed until he was comfy. I grabbed the knitted blanket from the armchair and threw it over him.

It must be hard being the brother of a sick sibling. I never really thought about how it affected him. I was always thinking about Bea, as I am sure everyone does. As a writer, I did realize, thinking back to all the time I had spent with them, that Jeremy always seemed to be a secondary character in the story. No one ever asked how he was doing, and he never ever complained about that or demanded attention. I guess tonight was his way of sharing his pain with someone.

I went up to my room and lay in bed, sleepless for what seemed like hours. I kept thinking about the imminent transplant my fiancé would need one day without warning. I had wanted to speak to Dr. Cooper earlier this evening and ask some questions of my own. I wanted to know more about transplantation and other alternatives. I'd checked Google and learned that they take 60 percent of the healthy donor liver, leaving 40 percent, which will regrow and is back to normal again within just a few months. The now 60 percent of the recipient's new liver then grows back to 100 percent. Obviously, there would be a fair amount of pain and a wicked scar, but I also learned that the outcomes for transplants were quite good. Many thoughts began to take shape in my head while I lay there, and I fell asleep with a very big idea on my mind.

I woke up in the morning and immediately checked my phone. Jeremy had sent me a text thanking me and letting me know he was already at the hospital. I jumped up and grabbed a baseball cap, threw on a pair of jeans, and rushed downstairs and out the door before anyone could stop me to ask questions. Once in my car, I sent a quick text to my mom, letting her know what was happening and that I would text her as soon as I knew more. I put the car into drive and tried not to speed.

Dr. Cooper was standing in the hallway, talking to Mr. and Mrs. Canning and Jeremy when I arrived. I approached them, and they all nodded at me while listening to the update. I tuned in as well, intent on getting as many answers as I could today.

". . . the greatest risk of this operation is transplant failure. In such a case, the body rejects the new liver, often for reasons no one can determine. A transplant also puts the patient at extremely high risk for infection, but we have many medications that work tremendously well."

Dr. Cooper spoke in a serious tone that only doctors seemed to have. "I know that this won't be the case here, but the number one cause of organ failure is the patient's failure to comply with the immunosuppression medical regimen. Bea will need to take a hefty and ongoing medication regimen for the rest of her life."

"Where does the new liver come from?" Brandon asked, putting his arms around Ria, who stared gravely at the floor.

"Organs are generally donated either from individuals who have been declared brain-dead and with the consent of their next of kin or from a living donor such as a relative or friend. Liver transplant centers match donors with recipients based on compatible liver size and blood type. The operation itself is major surgery, lasting between six and eight hours."

"And how do you decide when the time has come for Bea to have a transplant and who will be the donor?" Ria asked too softly.

Dr. Cooper confidently responded in a caring and patient tone, "The waiting time for a new liver may be uncertain and stressful. The sickest patients receive priority for a transplant. Prioritization is based on the severity of the liver disease measured by a model for end-stage liver disease score."

At this point, I only saw Dr. Cooper, Ria, and Brandon's lips moving. I noticed Jeremy had sat down a few feet away, stone sober now. I wondered how much of this information Bea knew. I pulled out my phone and checked to see if she was awake. I was dying to text her, but I would feel awful if I woke her up.

Bea: *Good morning! Sorry for the scare. I am doing great, don't worry. Feeling so happy and grateful for our amazing weekend. Just resting up for the big move next weekend. When do you want to pick out our new dog?*

Joel: *Hi, beautiful. Get better quickly so we can start our life together. What do you want to call him or her? What about Blue?*

Bea: *Blue, huh? Sounds perfect. I think Blue should be a boy. See you soon?*

Joel: *It's settled then, Blue it is. I am here now with your parents. Will come in as soon as they let me.*

The days passed, and so did Bea's fever and much of the strain and worry that had been etched on everyone's faces. After four days in hospital, Bea was more than ready to get out. I insisted on picking her up and bringing her home while our families worked together to make everything seem as normal as possible.

"Hey, babe!" I steered the wheelchair toward Bea's hospital bed, a blue stuffed dog under one arm. Bea's face lit up when she saw it. I handed it to her and kissed her on her head. "We'll work on the real thing as you get stronger."

"You're so sweet. I love it. Thank you." She clutched the stuffed dog to her chest and smiled up at me.

"Ready to get outta here?"

"Uh . . . yes!" Bea smiled radiantly. I helped her into the wheelchair and threw her overnight bag over one shoulder.

"How are you feeling today?" I asked as I wheeled her down the ICU hallway.

"Never better! Can we go visit Peter?"

"Sure, we can. He'd love to see you. Do you want to call your parents first?"

"Yes, and maybe we can stop by my mom's favorite flower shop. I would love to bring a beautiful bouquet home and one for your mom too. Does your mom like flowers? And how about Anna? Maybe we can swing by the chocolate shop too. Jeremy loves those peanut butter filled truffles."

"Whoa, slow down!" I laughed. "What have they been giving you in that place? You're like a runaway freight train!"

Bea giggled. "The prednisone makes me a bit overexcited. I am just feeling so great. It takes a lot out of a person to stay in bed for days on end, you know. I just want to get out and enjoy life again!"

I helped Bea into my car, kissing her while I buckled her up. It felt so good to have her with me again. As we drove, I thought of how easy it would be to just keep driving.

"Where would you like to go if we could just keep going?"

Bea turned to me, an expression of excitement on her face. "Well, I've always wanted to go to Lake Placid and go to the top of Whiteface Mountain for some beautiful sightseeing. Why?"

"Oh, just curious. What's the name of the flower shop again?"

"Maloney's Flowers," she answered distractedly while she looked outside. The roads were lined with gorgeous blooms of every color. An idea began to grow in my mind and while Bea got started in the flower shop, I made a few quick calls, promising I would be right in.

An hour later, my car was filled with three bouquets of flowers and several boxes of rich handmade chocolate truffles. We stopped for a chocolate shake at The Shake Shack and then dropped by to visit Peter. As we entered, carrying a large gold box of chocolates with a purple bow, one of the nurses crossing the expansive lobby walked up to us.

"Hi, Bea, Joel. Peter's having a nap right now, and Tess has gone out to do a little shopping. Would you like me to drop those off for them?"

"Yes, thank you," Bea said, handing the chocolates to her.

Next, we headed to Bea's. When we walked inside, everyone was there, even Anna and my parents. Ria came over, smiling, and hugged us both. "We were just about to have some lunch."

"Awesome, I'm starving," I said.

"Me too," Bea agreed, going into the dining room and sitting down.

The table was filled with potato salad, fresh buns, lunch meat, and an assortment of cheeses with all the fixings. We all sat down and chatted while making sandwiches and enjoying Ria's potato salad, which we all agreed was the best we have ever tried. My mom said she had to have the recipe, and Ria just smiled mysteriously.

"Bea, are you up for a drive when we're done?" I asked as she finished chewing a big bite of turkey sandwich.

"Really? We just got here," she said, surprised.

"Well, if you don't want to go to Lake Placid, we can go some other time, no problem."

A troubled look crossed Bea's face. "I'm not so sure that's a good idea, Joel." She stopped eating and stared down at her plate with an empty expression.

"I thought you said you'd love to go," I said, not understanding what just happened.

"You know, I'm really tired. I think I'm going to lie down," she said, excusing herself from the table. Everyone was silent as she left. Jeremy's eyebrows raised as he picked at his food. Anna stared at me as if trying to send a telepathic message.

Brandon spoke up, "Don't worry about it, son, this happens sometimes. Don't take it personally."

CHAPTER FOURTEEN

"Bea!" I whispered. I sat at the edge of her bed at her parents' place. She moved a few muscles. "Bea!" I whispered a little louder. "Wake up!" She began to stir, stretching her arms above her head and opening one blue eye.

"Joel?" she asked, confused.

"Come on, let's go for a drive. Wear something warm. It's a bit chilly outside."

"Where are we going?" she asked, sitting up in bed to look at me curiously.

"You'll see," I said, and I left her room to wait for her downstairs. I stood in the front foyer with Jeremy sitting in the living room, a cup of coffee in his hand.

"Does she know where you're taking her yet?" he asked.

"Not a clue," I replied. "I'm so excited. I hope this helps."

"I think it's a great idea," said Brandon, who came into the room neatly dressed in his usual shirt and sweater vest combo.

Bea appeared in an old washed out navy hoodie, a pair of ripped jeans, and her Converse high tops. Bea never seemed to care how she looked. I do not think I had ever even seen her look in a mirror, and I'd never seen anyone rock a pair of high tops the way she did. If I were a betting man, I would bet she would be wearing them the day we got married.

"What is so important that you had to interrupt my dream time?" she joked.

"You'll just have to wait and find out," I said, grabbing her hand. "Bye guys, she'll be back later," I called to Brandon and Jeremy. They both said goodbye and have fun, and we left.

"Where are we going, Joel?" Bea asked as we left town. "I've never seen you so excited."

"I'm not telling you."

"Why not?"

"Because this is too good of a surprise."

An hour later, we were in the country, enjoying the beautiful scenery. Bea was getting more confused by the minute. I was enjoying this so much. The past week had been hard, the hardest so far, in a way. Bea was shutting me out, and I thought I knew why. I imagined how I would feel in her place and realized how difficult it must be to feel like you are the cause of so much sorrow and worry.

I knew she felt like she was keeping me from living my life, and I knew there was really no way to explain to her how wrong she was. I would just have to show her, over time, that she was everything

I wanted. Of course, I had dreams, big dreams. I wanted to be a New York Times best-selling author, I wanted my books to become movies, I wanted a motorcycle and to travel to Greece and sail on the Adriatic Sea. But more than all of that, I wanted Bea.

We finally came to a large sign that read, "They're not good; they're Great . . . Danes!" I saw Bea's eyes widen into huge saucers. "No way! Oh my gosh!"

"They have puppies. I thought you would like to maybe pick one out. That is if you—"

Bea hopped out of the car the second it stopped and was jumping up and down with excitement. A tall, large man with a friendly smile came walking down the driveway. The sound of dogs barking was nearly deafening.

"You must be Joel and Bea. Welcome! I'm Doug," he said with an extended hand.

"Hi!" Bea and I said in unison. I shook his hand, and we followed him toward the back of his house where the kennel was located.

"The new pups are all ready for their new adventure," Doug said. "Most of them have homes already, but I have three of them still needing a family." He opened the door to the kennel and led us to a stall with silvery-blue Great Dane puppies eager to meet us. When Bea saw the puppies, she rushed toward them. I had never seen her smile so big.

"Oh, my God! Joel! Look at them. Aren't they amazing? Look at that one." She pointed to a puppy lying down calmly off to the side of the stall. He was looking at us and at his brothers and sisters who were all play fighting and nipping at each other's cute floppy ears. These were a breed called a Blue Great Dane, and they were amazing and huge. They each had a similar coat that appeared dark gray, and their eyes were all blue, just like Bea's.

"What do you think?" Doug said.

"I think they're amazing. I have to have one!"

"Look at that little guy in the corner," I said, pointing to the one keeping to himself. "He's pretty perfect, isn't he?"

"Really? Are you serious? Can we get him today?" Bea had this amazing way of thinking several thoughts all at once and blurting them out in no specific order.

I looked at Doug, who nodded with a grin. "Yep!"

I smiled. I was getting such a kick out of seeing this side of Bea. "They get pretty huge, though. Do you want to research the breed a bit? Or look at some others?"

I should have known better than to bother asking and watched Bea walk into the stall of complete mayhem and slowly lower herself to her knees in the center of the kennel to allow all the dogs a free for all. I did not know how she was not scared in the least, especially when the 120-pound mother came to check her out.

Bea looked back over her shoulder and gave me a look while she mouthed the words, "I love you."

My heart was overflowing. I watched as she waited patiently for Blue to get a little closer. I was feeling more and more delighted that I had come up with this idea as I knew this would be the perfect addition to our new little family and the perfect distraction during this time of change.

So much had happened this past year. Here we were, engaged to be married and moving into our dream home. Both of us had finished high school and were able to choose any path we wanted in life—well, sort of.

Thoughts of past conversations with Bea about travel, and many of the things she was no longer allowed to do because of her condition filled my mind. I could not help thinking of all the things that Bea couldn't do. Although I had no idea what it must have felt like to be Bea, I knew I had to keep trying to encourage her to focus on all the positives. There was no doubt that getting a puppy for Bea to take care of would help her feel like she had something new and exciting in her life while offering her more love than one person could handle. No one deserved this more than her.

Bea waited and waited while the other dogs jumped on her and tried licking her face. She just laughed and smiled and watched their antics with one eye on the object of her affection. She moved slowly but surely on her knees and got closer and closer to the shy puppy. Finally, he stuck his snout forward, straining his little furry neck to smell Bea's outstretched hand, and crouched forward little by little until he was close enough for her to place in her lap.

I went in to let him smell me too. The three of us sat on the floor for what seemed a long time until all the dogs had stretched out on top of one another to take a quick nap. Blue must have known he had found his new home. He was fast asleep in Bea's lap, snoring softly.

On the way home, Blue sat in the front on Bea's lap. He had been shaking so much we thought he would be less scared than in his crate in the back seat. I assured Bea we would take the back roads home and enjoy the drive and the lush scenery, with sprawling green pastures and picturesque hills and valleys surrounding us. The wide-open space made me feel lighter somehow. I had not realized how much stress I had been holding onto until we came out here, and the open roads and country air loosened the muscles in my shoulders and traps. I could get used to country living. As I drove, I snuck quick glances over at Bea, and she looked happier than I had seen her in a long time.

"Bea, I was just thinking about something. What if you made Blue a therapy dog? I think the American Kennel Club association has a dog therapy program. You could start bringing him in with you when you volunteer at the retirement home." I knew I had hit on something when Bea looked at me with excitement.

"What an amazing idea! I love that. How do you come up with this stuff?" Bea reached for my hand, and we enjoyed the soft snoring noise coming from Bea's lap.

"Have you thought of what we need to get for Blue?"

"Why don't you grab your phone, and we can start a list right now."

"Sure. Okay, we'll need a good leash and a bed to place in his crate, and he should probably stay in the kitchen most of the time, so we'll need a gate for the doorway. I bet he'll be scared with all the space, so keeping his crate in the kitchen with the door open so he can come and go when he pleases should help. Oh, and our old neighbor used to have a dog who loved this little rubbery thing, I think it's called a Kong. She used to put peanut butter in it and yogurt and then freeze it, and it helped when her dog was teething as a pup. This is going to be so much fun. That reminds me, are you all ready to move in? Only two days to go."

"I was born ready," I joked with Bea. "Bea, I'm ready as long as you are beside me. I'd follow you anywhere and probably do anything if it would make you happy."

"Better be careful what you say, Joel. What if I ask you to jump out of an airplane? Or go bungee jumping? I do not have to listen to the doctors, you know. What are you going to do then? Huh?"

I laughed, relieved to have my Bea back. I had not seen her in a good mood since our special weekend together. "I'm up for anything," I said reassuringly. "Just name it."

"Okay, it's on." Bea looked deep in thought. "Have you thought about how you want our wedding to go?"

"Of course, I have. All I want is for you to be happy and feeling good," I said, squeezing her hand. "Oh, and I hope you don't get cold feet."

"Well, I mean, I can't now," she said playfully, pointing to Blue. "We have a fur baby now. Can't break up his family!" She kissed him on the head.

"How are you feeling?" I asked. "Are you getting used to the new meds?"

Bea seemed somewhat deflated by this question, but still, she answered. "Yeah, I guess. I feel pretty irritated sometimes, and I don't have much of an appetite."

"I know we haven't talked much about, you know, needing a transplant, but I'm here, okay? If you ever need to talk about it."

"It's pretty weird," she said, shaking her head and turning to look out the window. "I know that they know what they're doing, and lots of people get them. It's just so weird to think about having somebody else's organ inside of me, especially someone who might be dead. And it is a little scary thinking that they wait until the last minute. I mean, what if they cannot find one? I do not want any of my family going through a major surgery like that. Jeremy faints just going to the dentist."

"It must be scary. Just think, though, Bea. Wouldn't you want to give one of your organs to someone to save their life? I think it's the most unbelievable gift there is."

"Yeah, it's amazing, and I'd be forever grateful to the person who gives me that gift."

"What if I gave you part of my liver?"

"Wow," she said quietly. "What did I do to deserve you?"

"Are you kidding me? You are the most beautiful, giving soul I know. And I would do absolutely anything for you. You do know that, don't you?"

"Yes, I do. But I would never want you to go through that kind of pain for me. Who knows if you'd even be able to?"

"Well, I want to find out, just in case. I already talked to Jeremy and Anna about it. We all want to find out if we can be donors. Who knows, maybe we will be able to help someone else. We only need, like, one kidney, right? Maybe I can donate my kidney to someone and save them. That would be amazing."

"You're nuts, you know that? Crazzzzzyyyyyy!"

"I'm crazy in love with you. That's what I am!"

CHAPTER FIFTEEN

Late in the summer, I started reflecting on my life, how my dreams had begun to take shape, as did what I wanted to come next. I wanted to be a writer. I had known it all my life, from the time I was a small child. My mother started reading to Anna and me when we were a day old. She would lie down between us and read. We saw lots of pictures of us in her special family albums, and there was never a page without one of us holding a book.

I loved taking an idea of a quirk or characteristic from a person, whether real or fictional and developing it into a character in my imagination. Did this character like pizza, the color orange, summer over autumn? Did he prefer salty over sweet, beach or mountains?

I have had many book ideas over the years and have finished a few stories. I enjoy the dramatic fiction genre the best, a prose or verse composition that presents in dialogue and action a story involving conflict or contrast of characters. I have never shown anyone my work, aside from essays and a few short stories I had written in school. I was almost finished with a novel that would be the first work that I send out to the world.

I had been collecting information on how to submit a manuscript to publishers and had learned the Catch-22 that seemed to exist in so many areas of life. To get a publisher interested in your book, you must use a literary agent to submit the work. And literary agents only take a limited number of clients. It was frustrating. There is also the less traditional route of self-publication, but I did not want to do the work required to market the book. All I wanted to do was write.

I cannot imagine any other job. Writing would not even be a job. Isn't a job something where you trade your time for money, and you work hard and never really get ahead? Maybe not, but that is what it seemed like to me. If you do not love what you are doing, what is the point? For me, writing is my passion, hobby, and relaxation. The only thing more amazing than writing is writing while I'm with Bea.

I was preparing dinner for us on the Monday of Labor Day weekend before my first day of university. Bea loved to eat healthy, especially now since she had resumed her jogging, against the recommendations of her doctors. We all knew better than to challenge Bea when she had her mind set. She had made it clear to all of us that this was her life, and she was not going to eliminate everything she loved because of a chance that something could happen.

I wanted to surprise Bea with a new recipe my mom had taught me. The dish was called bulgogi and had all the elements of eating that Bea seemed to love best. Bulgogi was chicken breast sautéed in a mixture of Chinese flavorings, sprinkled with sesame seeds, and served on sticky rice. The entire mixture is placed inside of a leaf of butter lettuce and wrapped up like a fajita.

I wanted to show her how much I appreciated all the time she was spending organizing our new home and training Blue. He was a handful, that is for sure, but we loved him and could not imagine not having him. Even the ducks loved him as they would chase each other around the pond.

Our moms and my sister had spent the day with Bea planning and discovering ideas for our wedding. Bea wanted it all to be a surprise for me, and I did not mind one bit. She had amazing taste, and I could just imagine how perfect she would make it.

As it turned out, the pizza delivery guy was happy with the tip I gave him and smiled as he smelled the burned food emanating from the kitchen.

"I think I'll need a few lessons in the kitchen," I said when Bea came home to the smell of burned chicken. She just laughed and said, "Pizza?" And, after scraping at my frying pan one last time, I reluctantly agreed. After dinner, I spent a few hours writing while Bea lounged in the luxurious bubble bath I had drawn for her.

"You better not get tired of spoiling me, Joel, because I'm going to expect that we do sweet things for each other for the rest of our lives, you know. So, get used to it."

"I promise I will always spoil you."

"Good. I want the romance to continue every day."

"Well, you've chosen the right guy. You should read some of the romantic stuff I come up with in my journal and writing."

"How's your book going, by the way?"

"It's going amazingly well. I cannot believe I'm writing a romance novel. I didn't know I had it in me."

Bea and I cuddled on the couch with Blue later and watched a movie that made me cry. I had never cried at a movie before. Probably because Mom and Anna watched the chick flicks together while Dad and I played catch or went for drives. I will admit that I was really missing out. This movie really got to me, though, and I wondered why Bea liked it as much as she did. I mean, it was sweet and romantic, but it was also extremely sad. I had wondered about this long into the night while she slept beside me, her head on my chest. Maybe there was consolation in knowing that others were worse off.

It was so amazing living with Bea. We were so fortunate that our parents accepted our decision. Some might think that in a perfect world, we would have waited until we got married, but neither of us wanted to wait because we didn't know what the future held. Although we had been as close as a couple can be, and both of us had what I believed to be a healthy outlook on sex, we were not in any rush to prove anything to each other. I loved exploring Bea's body and soul at the same time. Even though Bea had a few scars here and there from her biopsies, she was stunningly beautiful and confident with her body.

Time was passing by quickly, and school was more demanding than I had thought. Of course, I knew it would be a lot of work. Bea was great about getting things done around the house, although I often wondered if she was overdoing it. Bea was a type-A personality, just like my mom. Neither of them ever stopped and seemed to wake up early and go, go, go all day until late at night.

Bea had signed up to run a 10K on Halloween and spent an hour or more training every day. On top of that, she took Blue for two to three walks each day, took care of his training, made meals, and still found time to volunteer at Tess and Peter's retirement home, along with spending her usual time with Peter.

Sometimes Bea looked a funny color, a pale yellow, but whenever I pointed it out, she denied it. It was not until I had developed a bad headache and left my afternoon Literature and Society class that I had accidentally stumbled upon something that led to our first argument.

I arrived home and quietly walked into the kitchen, opening the cupboard where we kept the Tylenol. Bea was not allowed to take any medication other than her regular regime of meds, so I was concerned when I did not find the bottle. Blue opened one eye and twitched his nose, and when he was sure it was me, he fell back asleep. Bea must have taken him for a long walk and tired him out. Curious, I walked toward our bedroom. There, on our bed, buried in blankets, was Bea, fast asleep, the Tylenol bottle left open beside her on the nightstand.

My mind began to race as I wondered what might be going on. Was Bea alright? Was she in pain and keeping it from me? Was sleeping all day while I was at school a regular thing she did? I could not help wondering if the reason why Bea seemed to have an endless reserve of energy was because she slept all day. I quietly left the room and lay down on the sofa.

"Wake up!"

I opened my eyes and looked into foreign eyes that seemed to emit a death glare full of anger and hostility.

"What are you doing home? Don't you have class? Were you checking up on me?" Bea fired questions at me one after another.

"I came home early because I had a headache." I sat up uncertainly, anger roiling up through me from being on the receiving end of her unjustified hostility.

Bea was pacing back and forth, and Blue was whining quietly in the corner, uncomfortable with the tension between us. This was a foreign feeling for us all.

"Bea, what's the matter with you? Why were you sleeping, and why are you taking Tylenol? I thought you were only supposed to take it if you absolutely had to?"

Bea continued to pace back and forth, looking up once or twice to glare at me.

"Bea, why don't you sit down for a second and tell me what's going on."

"I don't want to sit down. All you do is worry about every little thing I do. You are just like everyone else. I cannot do anything normal without everybody losing it and getting concerned looks on their faces. I mean, do you think I don't notice you staring at me all the time? God, I cannot do anything. I have to sleep so that I can keep everyone satisfied that I'm doing fine."

I had never seen Bea like this. I had watched her frustrated and seen her vacillate between moods and came to understand the rhythm of things. This was very different. She was out of control.

"Bea, just talk to me, okay? I see you are upset. I want to listen. Just tell me what you're feeling right now."

Bea burst into tears, sobbing uncontrollably. "I feel like everything is out of control. I don't know how to stop it. Everything in my life is amazing and perfect, except for my insides. I can feel my body getting sicker, and I try to ignore it and stay positive and remind myself of all the things I can do, but every minute of every day, I am so tired. I'm so tired, Joel."

My heart broke, seeing her like this. I gently guided her to the couch and put my arm around her shoulders. We stayed like that, remaining quiet. Bea was not much of a crier, and so she wiped her tears and looked at me sadly.

"I don't know what to do," she said.

"Do you want me to take you to see your doctor? Are you in pain?"

"I don't feel great, to be honest."

"How long has this been going on?"

"A while. I didn't want to say anything. You're working so hard on your manuscript and school, and everyone is trying so hard to plan our wedding and getting this place set up and doing all these amazing things for us. I don't want to let anyone down. And I am so tired of everyone tiptoeing around me, and that look in everyone's eyes, like 'poor Bea' and being so overprotective. I know everyone is just being caring and loving me, but I just so badly want to be normal. I want to jump on a plane with you and go to Mexico and just walk around for hours on the beach and swim in the ocean. I can't. Bea can't do this or do that! I am just so tired of it all and just so tired in general. All I want to do is sleep and stop pretending that I am feeling good and have energy. The truth is that I don't!"

My heart broke, and I felt completely helpless. There was nothing I could do. This was a new sensation for me. There would never be anything I could do but love her and support her.

I tried to imagine what it must be like to be her, every day wondering what my body is doing. I felt so angry with her body and how it was trying to attack and kill her liver. I'd learned the liver was responsible for many functions, the main one being filtering and cleaning the body. The liver also plays a central role in fat metabolism and producing energy.

Bea looked at me, longingly. "You can't imagine how bad I feel for you, and for Jeremy and my parents. You do not need this. You could have any girl, a healthy one who can be carefree and go anywhere and do anything with you. Did you know that even if the transplant works, I am still always going to need to take tons of meds, have a million doctor's appointments and that it can come back? I cannot even imagine having somebody else's organ in my body. How gross. I'm going to feel like Frankenstein."

"Bea, your family lives life to the fullest because of you. And as for me, you are the most wonderful person I have ever known. I never expected that falling in love, being in love, could ever be this amazing. I cannot even breathe without you. Every day you teach me how to love, how to appreciate all the small things in life and the big things. Colors seem brighter, food tastes better, water is wetter. I sound like an idiot, but it's true. You have just got to believe me. I would not trade you in for anything on this earth. I thank God every night for you, and I ask myself every minute how I can be so incredibly lucky to have you. I'm even writing a book with you as one of my main characters."

I let my words sink in, and then I kissed her.

"Let's call Dr. Cooper and see what he says. It's better to deal with this head-on and not sweep anything under the rug. Okay? No matter what happens, we are still getting married and having kids and living an incredible life. You just need to get used to that and the fact that you are stuck with me. Got it?"

"No. But I'll keep trying."

Bea talked me into making her dinner before calling Dr. Cooper. After that, she excused herself to take a quick shower and to pack a few things in her overnight bag in case she needed to be admitted. I saw a new look on her face. This time, instead of looking sick and tired, she now looked exhausted and scared. I could not help wondering if she knew on some level that things had gotten tremendously out of hand.

When she did not return, I went in to see what was keeping her and found her fast asleep under the covers, a deep crease etched on her forehead. I decided waiting until morning could not hurt. I spent the remainder of the evening at my desk researching liver transplants. There was a lot of great information that put my mind at rest, even though my heart ached.

In the morning, after getting the coffee going and taking Blue for a much-needed short walk, I returned home to find that the house was quiet. Much too quiet. I called for Bea as I walked toward our room. I hoped she did not think she was going to get away with not calling Dr. Cooper. I was surprised to see that she was still sound asleep. I sat down gingerly beside her, staring at her for a few moments before shaking her gently.

"Bea, wake up!"

She opened her eyes, and I felt my heart plummet as I saw her eyes.

"Bea, you need to get up." I did not want to startle her, but the fear in my eyes must have given away what I had seen. Bea sat up and cried silently. She did not say a word as she got up and walked toward Blue's crate.

"Bye boy, I promise I'll be back soon." Since she was still wearing her jogging pants and hoody from yesterday, she slipped on her flip flops and turned to me and said, "Okay, let's go."

I grabbed her overnight bag and got into the car. Bea assured me that she had texted her parents, who I assumed would be meeting us at the hospital. I tried my best to keep my eyes in front of me while we drove the short distance to the hospital. The color yellow became my least favorite color until the end of time.

CHAPTER SIXTEEN

Bea was admitted to the hospital as soon as they looked at her. I could not believe how fast this illness had progressed to the next level. Dr. Cooper said that many patients with the same illness live years before needing a transplant, but for some unknown reason, Bea's body did not want to cooperate.

"Bea, how are you feeling? Are you in any pain?" Dr. Cooper asked. He seemed concerned and less easygoing than usual.

"It hurts here." She pointed to her liver.

"Have you been lethargic?"

"Yes, very."

"Appetite?"

"Terrible."

Dr. Cooper began to examine Bea's arms and legs.

"How long have you had these?" he asked, pointing to some red marks on Bea's arms and legs.

"I hadn't noticed them. Joel? Did you?" She looked at me.

I shook my head. "What are they?"

"Bea, we are going to need to run some tests to see where we are. These marks are called spider angiomas, abnormal blood vessels on the skin. What about these bruises?" He pointed to her legs.

"I'm always bumping into things, especially now that we have Blue, our new puppy." Bea smiled as she said Blue's name.

"Bea, is there any chance you're pregnant?"

"Well, yes, but we've been very careful."

Dr. Cooper continued to ask more and more questions, which put us more and more on edge.

"How has your memory been?"

"I don't know. I forget things just like everyone else, I think."

Dr. Cooper turned to me. "Joel, what do you think?"

"Well," I said, looking nervously from Dr. Cooper to Bea. "There have been times lately where Bea has forgotten to pick up the dry cleaning, and once she forgot a pot of boiling water on the stove. She also forgot to meet me for lunch once recently. I didn't say anything to her."

I glanced nervously at Bea, who looked a little surprised. "I thought that she was just getting used to living with me and excited about our wedding."

Dr. Cooper continued to take Bea's vitals. "Bea, I notice you're scratching. Is that new?"

"Fairly new, I guess. I thought maybe I was just getting used to Blue."

The grave look on Dr. Cooper's face made me feel sick. His usual calming presence had been replaced with a serious tone and extra lines on his face.

Brandon, Ria, and Jeremy arrived within the hour. They each took turns giving her a hug and then stood by, their shoulders tense.

"So, what exactly is going on?" Brandon asked with a furrowed brow.

"Well, we are going to run a few more tests to confirm," Dr. Cooper said to the group. "But I feel as though we've come to the point where we need to do a liver transplant." He said it like ripping off a bandage, and the room seemed to go quiet. Even the nearby nurses' station hushed at those words. You could hear our breathing speed up and as the quiet continued, so too did the strain and worry. Bea looked at her parents, at me, and then at Jeremy and tried to force a smile.

"Well, we knew this day was coming," she said bravely. "Let's do it."

Bea looked at Dr. Cooper and asked, "How much time do I have to prepare?"

"Bea, I think it's amazing that you have such a great attitude. It's really going to help you get through this," Dr. Cooper said cautiously. "I want you to know that we are most likely going to need a liver in the next twenty-four to forty-eight hours."

Bea sobered up quickly, hearing the time frame. Everything we had heard before from the team of doctors was that at the point when Bea needed a transplant, it would be twenty-four to forty-eight hours or imminent death.

This could not be happening. I felt like my heart was going to burst out of my chest, and they would have to wheel me into one of the operating rooms. We were supposed to get married in three weeks, on December twentieth, the anniversary of the day I told Bea I loved her for the first time, under the moon that matched the necklace I'd given her that day.

I looked up at Bea, who sat motionless, her eyes and skin radiating a sickly yellow color. I looked over at Brandon, Ria, and Jeremy and saw their expressions, fearful and colorless.

Jeremy clutched his stomach, his face pale and sweaty. "Sorry," he said quickly as he suddenly bolted for the nearby washroom.

"So, what's next, Dr. Cooper?" Bea asked, bravery still in her soft voice.

The truth was that Bea was probably the only one of us who was ready for this. Everyone who loved her prayed and hoped that this day would never come. But for Bea, she probably hoped and prayed that it would come. At least she had a shot at being healthier with a new liver, although she would need to adopt a heavy new medication regime. Regardless of whether we were ready, the day was here. I had thought about this long and hard, and I knew what I needed to do.

"Bea, Mr. and Mrs. Canning, I spoke to Dr. Cooper the last time Bea was admitted, and we ran some tests. I'm a match."

Ria put her hands to her mouth while Brandon stood there in shock.

"I'd like to donate a piece of my liver." I looked deep into Bea's eyes as I said this, knowing the weight of my words, knowing all I had just agreed to.

Ria took a quick intake of breath and started sobbing. Brandon held her in his arms, his own face wet with tears.

"Bea, this is something I decided a long time ago," I said. "I'm aware of all the risks, and there's nothing you can say that will change my mind. This is our battle, and we'll fight it together."

"Joel, you are . . . you are . . . ." She buried her face in her hands.

"I've already discussed it with my parents and sister, and they are totally supportive. I love you. We're going to finish this." I hugged her in her wheelchair and let her cry on my shoulder while I patted her reassuringly. "We've got this. You and me. We're going to be closer than you ever dreamed!"

Bea's face was buried into my shirt, but I thought I heard a giggle through the tears. Then she pulled away, and she was smiling and laughing. The laughter grew until I started laughing.

"What?" I said, trying not to laugh at a time like this. But Bea would not stop. She was howling. Then Ria started laughing, and my laughter got even worse. Even Brandon let out a few chuckles.

"Joel," he said as we quieted down. "We will be forever grateful, son. You are the greatest blessing our family has received, and we are so thankful that our daughter," he choked, as more tears came, "has found true and honest love. It's all a father could ever hope for his daughter." Then he turned away and walked a few steps to collect himself.

I held Bea, who was still smiling, and rubbed her arm encouragingly. "We've got this," I whispered.

Over the course of the evening, once Bea's test results confirmed Dr. Cooper's prognosis, things began to move fast. First, I contacted my family, who assured me they would be here first thing in the morning, a few hours before the surgery time.

Next, I was admitted, and a bed was brought into Bea's room for me. I was visited by several nurses and the anesthesiologist, who all asked me the regular questions about allergies and previous surgeries.

A few hours later, after everyone's questions had been answered thoroughly, the Cannings were about to go home.

"Can someone call Peter and Tess?" Bea asked. It was so like her to be worrying about others while her life was in jeopardy. "Mom, please see if Peter can come by in the morning if it's at all possible. I know he's not very mobile, but it would mean a lot."

"Of course, dear. I will call him on the way home. Don't you worry." Ria turned to me now. "Joel, we don't know how to thank you. We can never repay you for what you are willing to do for our beautiful daughter. You have touched our hearts forever, and we can't wait for you both to have so many happy memories together."

I could see it all in her eyes as she looked to the very depths of my soul.

Jeremy was about to give me a fist bump and, at the last minute, pulled me into a hug. Mr. and Mrs. Canning both hugged me too.

They each hugged and kissed Bea, telling her how much they loved her and reassuring her that everything would turn out alright. Jeremy hugged her very tightly, longer than their parents. He whispered something to her that I did not hear, and then he pulled away and walked out of the room. With one last goodbye, Bea's parents left as well.

Once alone together, Bea looked uncomfortably shy. I was feeling strange myself. But this is what I wanted, and it had to happen now. Life did not wait for me to meet Bea when I thought I would, and it would not wait now. Life did whatever it wanted to when it wanted to. There was no rhyme or reason to any of it. It just was. Bea needed a new liver, and I had one to share.

Bea had asked me to give her a moment while she closed her eyes. Almost immediately, she began snoring softly. I was hooked up to an IV and blood pressure cuff but wanted to be close to Bea. I removed the blood pressure cuff, slipped out of my bed, and wheeled the pole with the IV fluids over to where Bea lay fast asleep. I gently climbed up into her bed and lay down beside her.

Wow. This was really happening. I wish I had my journal. Instead, I closed my eyes and pictured Bea and me getting married. I fell asleep with the image of her looking so beautiful, standing barefoot under the light of the moon, her white silk dress clinging to her curves. Her long, curly hair was wild as it flowed softly in the light wind. She wore no makeup and held one long-stemmed white calla lily, her favorite.

The morning came and not a moment too soon. Staying overnight in a hospital sucked. The nurses would come in every two hours and take our vitals. They made me promise each time that I would return to my bed, and each time I promised but did not. I wanted to be close to Bea in case she woke up and freaked out. She slept all through the night and was still sleeping. Her skin looked even more yellow this morning. I was afraid to see her eyes. Before long, both of our families had gathered in the room. Bea continued to sleep. We all thought it best to let her sleep, and we just talked quietly until Dr. Cooper arrived.

"So, how are my favorite patients?" Dr. Cooper asked as he entered the room.

Bea seemed dead to the world.

"I'm doing fine. Bea has been asleep for hours. Do you think she's okay?"

"Bea?" Dr. Cooper called loudly. When she did not respond, he shook her awake. "Okay, Miss Canning, time to wake up and join us."

Bea slowly began to stir, wincing painfully when she moved. Her eyes shot open. They were blue and yellow, almost appearing green. It made me feel nauseous to look at them.

"Ow!" she said louder than expected. "It hurts. My abdomen, it hurts, bad."

Dr. Cooper walked to the door, summoned a nurse, and asked for him to bring a few different medications I had not heard of before. He began examining Bea's eyes, arms, and legs. When the nurse who had been on duty all night, Cody, came in, Dr. Cooper proceeded to give him further instructions. He also asked him to contact the transplant team. Cody administered some new meds through Bea's IV and gave her a wink. He had been so great to us the entire night.

When Bea felt the effects of the pain meds, she seemed to relax a bit, and we were all relieved. The rest of the team of surgeons arrived and introduced themselves just as Peter and Tess slowly shuffled into the room. Peter looked like he was a total mess. He was obviously scared and quietly kissed Bea on the cheek and squeezed her hand.

"I'll be here when you wake up, my love," he said to her softly.

The time finally came, and the doctors alerted us that they were ready.

"I love you guys," Bea said without crying. "I'll see you soon." The way she said this was so firm and determined, reminding me why I loved her so much, reminding me that despite the fear I felt, I was determined for her too.

"We love you too," Ria said, looking unsteady on her feet.

"Let's all pray," Brandon said, extending his hands to his wife and daughter. We all joined hands and bowed our heads with eyes closed as he spoke. "Lord, watch over my daughter and my son-in-law today as they go into surgery. Be with them, be with the surgeons as they work, and give our children back to us alive and well. I thank you for how blessed we are to have each other and for the wonderful privilege of being the father of such a fiercely strong woman. I ask you to give us all strength today. Amen."

Bea's family surrounded her in a hug, hard expressions on all their faces.

I looked at my own family, and they stared back with both sadness and hope in their eyes. "Hey Mom, why don't we have homemade pizza this weekend. We can have a competition to see who can make the best one."

My mom looked like she might burst into tears, but she pulled herself together and smiled. "Sounds great, honey."

"Girls against the boys?" I asked, nudging Anna.

She gave me a hug. "We'll crush you," she said gently.

We all laughed.

Jeremy caught my eye and gave me a small smile as he moved closer and leaned in for a one-armed hug. "You got this, bro!"

Bea was wheeled out first and then me, and I looked back at our loved ones and smiled. They all shared their love through their eyes until they were out of sight. We were wheeled down the hall, into the elevators, and brought to sit just outside of our operating rooms.

"Can I say a few words to Bea before we go in?" I asked the nurses who were standing by, their masks covering their faces.

"Of course," Bea's nurse answered gruffly, trying not to show any emotion. They went a few feet away to give us a moment alone.

I reached over and held Bea's hand. "Bea, I love you. With every cell in my body, I love you. You are everything to me. Please be strong and know that I am here, and I will be here when you wake up. We have the rest of our lives ahead of us, and I'm so thankful I found you."

Bea squeezed my hand and said, "I love you too. I will never be able to explain how grateful I am. It's hard to believe that I met you by mere chance, that you just happened to move to my street, and you happened to be not just my soulmate," she paused, unable to continue. Tears finally streamed down her face after being absent all morning. "You are the one who would save my life as well."

I leaned over my bed to kiss her gently.

"See you soon," I said, smiling.

She smiled back. "See you soon."

The nurses came for us, and we were both rolled into separate rooms and prepared for the surgery.

It was so cold that I was shaking. I thought of Bea and how much she hated air conditioning and smiled to myself. I loved that girl.

"Please, God, take care of her and watch over her," I whispered, looking up at the ceiling. The nurse put the mask over my face and told me to count down from ten. I think I only got to seven, my lucky number.

CHAPTER SEVENTEEN

I opened one eye, then the next, and looked around the room as I came to consciousness. My throat burned, and I could feel the breathing tube was still attached, I suppose in case there are any complications. Jeremy's face appeared for a quick moment to look through the window of the ICU room, and it looked like he had been crying. I saw our parents just beyond him, talking with a nurse. It looked like they were crying too.

My breathing was coming in shallow gasps, and the pain I was feeling was so sharp and intense that it nearly took my breath away. I could hear my mom from the other side of the door as she noticed me stirring.

"Oh my God, Bea. She is okay, Brandon! Oh, thank you, God!" My mom looked up toward the sky, clasping her hands together as she said her thanks.

"I'll let Dr. Cooper know," Jeremy said, disappearing down the hall.

Moments later, I saw Dr. Cooper appear. Before coming into my room, he acknowledged my family somberly. I heard him tell them my room was off-limits to everyone but hospital staff for the next two days. Lucky me. He came into the room and smiled at me, although it seemed like a sad smile.

"Hey Bea, I know you're feeling a lot of pain right now," he said gently. "It's important for you to stay calm and try to control your breathing. Do not try to talk, either, as we have a breathing tube inserted into your trachea. I know it feels like you have an elephant sitting on your chest, and your throat is most likely very sore. I am going to hand you this pump right here. It is a self-administering morphine pump. Do not worry. You cannot overdose by using it, but it will help to control your pain. I know you want to see your family, but please rest. You need to sleep to let your body heal and accept your new liver. We will be checking on you often. You are not alone. Sleep now."

I looked at him appreciatively without a sound as instructed. Dr. Cooper turned and left my room quietly, returning to my family outside the door. He regarded them with a satisfied look on his face, and I could hear him say, "Well, let us keep our fingers crossed, shall we? I know you want to stay close, but Bea needs to sleep as much as she can right now. I would go home and get some rest. You're all going to need it."

Over the next two days, as I moved in and out of sleep, I would worry about my family, imagining my parents and Jeremy spending the day pacing back and forth, probably unsure of what to do next. I recalled the shocked looks on their faces after I woke up as if they were trying to make sense of things. I wondered if they had visited with Joel, who the nurse told me was in a room down the hall. I thought about Joel and would gently touch my bandages where beneath my skin, a part of his liver was now. He had saved me.

I would sometimes wake up with a gasp, my heart racing, and then I would think of Joel and remember that this was the turning point. I could get better now, thanks to him. I would get to do so many of the things I had spent years wondering if I'd ever be able to experience. I could not wait to do them with Joel. I still wanted to get married on December twentieth, our special day, even if we were both in wheelchairs for the ceremony. I missed him so much and realized I had not gone this long without seeing him since we had first met.

When I was awake, I thought about his beautiful face, the feeling I got when he kissed me and replayed all our memories. I thought about the electricity I felt from his skin the first time we shook hands and how much I couldn't wait to marry this incredible man. He was young, but I could not think of a more wise, strong, determined, compassionate, or kind person. I had been in love with him from the moment I met him. I knew that no matter what happened, Joel would be there, and everything would be okay. I wanted a lifetime with him and knew that I was better because of him. It was the kind of love that lets you know—like a warning—that if you were to get to know this person, he would consume your every thought and make every moment you spend without him seem pointless.

That was Joel. When I looked into his eyes for the first time, after he nearly crashed into me on his skateboard, I could hear the warning bells chiming in my brain. For months I spent time with him, reading, talking, learning about one another, and those warning bells were always there. While my brain told me to be careful, my heart was saying otherwise. My body responded to his movements, and I felt a sense of safety and freedom I had never felt with anyone else, not even Peter or my family.

I guess I sort of knew the whole time that he was the one for me. It just took me and my logical thinking some time to get used to the idea. I realized that I did not need to look because he had already found me. He was like an angel sent from heaven. He offered me pure happiness and made my future seem exciting for the first time since I was diagnosed. Alone, I felt like I was sick and stuck. Joel made me believe I could fight this disease and that I could have a normal happy life with him if I had his hand to hold onto.

Finally, on the third day after my surgery, my tube was removed, and my parents could visit me. They walked into my room and stood motionless without speaking. They looked strange and very worried.

"Mom, Dad! How are you? Come check out my eyes. One of the nurses brought me a mirror so I could see. Look, they are white!"

They approached my bed, tentatively, my dad holding onto a small stuffed bear.

"Where's Jer?"

"Your brother's just getting a drink from the vending machine. He'll be right back," my mom said. "How are you feeling?"

"Well, it hurts more than I expected, and I feel like I'm constantly drifting in and out, but I feel stronger. I am not itchy anymore. Where's Joel? I thought I saw him watching me sleep a few times, but the nurses said I was probably only dreaming. He's got his own room down the hall?"

My parents each took a step closer to me, my mom on my left and my dad on my right. I felt a panicky feeling begin to surface, unsure of what was happening. Why did my mom look so upset? She looked as though she were bracing herself for something terrible that was about to happen.

"Bea, there's no easy way to say this, honey." She looked at my dad for support, her eyes brimming with tears.

My body tensed. "Mom, Dad . . . is it Peter? Oh no. Did something happen to him?"

"No, Peter and Tess are both fine," my dad replied.

"Then what? You both look like someone died. Did the transplant not work or something? Did they find something else? Cancer? What is it?"

The sick feeling of worry intensified as my intuition finally caught up with me in one devastating moment. I clasped onto the guard rails on either side of my bed, pain slicing through my body. This time, the pain was of a very different kind, the kind of pain that made me want to close my eyes forever.

"Dad," I tried to speak, but the lump that had lodged in my throat was cutting off my breath. I was starting to get dizzy, and my breathing became rapid. The machines attached to me were beeping erratically, and I could feel my heart rate speed up like my heart would pop right out of my chest. I started panting as I searched my parents' faces for the answers I needed but did not want.

"Where is Joel?" I gasped. "Is he okay?"

Tears streamed down my mother's face, and my dad covered his eyes, his brow furrowed in pain.

"Bea," my mom managed to get out. "Joel had an allergic reaction to the anesthesia. He went into anaphylactic shock during the surgery. Joel's . . . honey, he's in a coma."

I felt my insides trying to burst from my skin and warm liquid rushing through my body like a wave. I fought the tears trying to come out and forced my voice to be steady. "He's going to be okay, though." I said this as a statement and not a question, as if I could change the words I was about to hear into what I wanted.

"Bea," my dad continued, "my sweetheart," he choked on his words, crying freely. "Joel is not going to wake up. He was deprived of oxygen and . . . ." He stopped and looked at me.

The machines buzzed wildly, and two nurses ran in and began adjusting the monitors. Without warning, I felt like a giant lead blanket dropped on me, and my lungs had collapsed.

"What's happening?" my mom cried.

"She might pass out, but she's stable," one of the nurses said.

They say that the most painful goodbyes are the ones that are never said and never explained. There is no way to describe the pain I felt at that moment, and then all at once, everything disappeared.

Chapter Eighteen

I could see Joel a couple of days after I found out. I asked my favorite nurse, Cody, to take me at night after visiting hours were over, and I would be sure not to bump into any of his family. I just could not face them. They must hate me so much. Anna lost her twin for God's sake.

The pain I felt, not just for myself but for his family, was unbearable. When I slept, it was as if the effects of rest did not work on my body. I felt debilitated with exhaustion all day, and all night I tossed and turned. I felt sick every waking moment, a pit in my stomach, leaving me feeling raw and weak.

I had learned from Cody that the Petersons had allowed Joel to remain on a ventilator for me so that I could say goodbye. I was so grateful. I could hardly believe they would do that, especially since I was the reason for their loss.

My parents tried telling me that Joel had been set on this from the start and wanted nothing more than to give me his liver. I knew deep down that this was true, but the constant ache in my heart was agonizing. This brought a whole new kind of pain into my life, and it literally made me feel like I was being tormented every moment of the day.

When I was finally in front of him, it was as if it were not true. He looked like he was just sleeping, and if I were to reach for his hand, his green eyes would slowly open, and he would be smiling at me, ready to make me laugh. I looked at his handsome face, at the way his dark hair curled slightly at the tips, and he looked so peaceful that it seemed impossible that he would never wake up. I wondered if he could see me, hear me from wherever he was. I took his hand in mine and stared at it. I had loved his hands so much. I pictured them cupping my face when he kissed me, petting Blue, helping Peter up from his chair, writing. They were perfect hands, meant to write and create beauty and wonder in the world.

"Joel, I'm so sorry. I love you so much." I sat with him for an hour or more, just holding onto his hand. I did not know what else to say. I knew that tomorrow, Joel would be disconnected from the tubes, and he would officially be dead.

I could not stop staring at him, the color in his cheeks, the warmth in his body, but he was not there anymore. This body in front of me looked like my Joel, and I could almost catch myself thinking things like, *when he wakes up*, or *in two weeks when we get married*, or *I should buy flowers for our home*. It was too much to bear.

I slowly stood from my wheelchair, leaned painfully toward Joel's face, and kissed his lips. "I love you, Joel. I'll love you forever. Thank you for loving me." I sat back down in my chair and wheeled myself away, looking over my shoulder one final time to imprint his face into my mind forever.

All day long, as I lay in my hospital bed getting poked and prodded by doctors and nurses, I found myself checking my phone, expecting to hear from him any moment. I expected him to walk down the hall and come into my room to hold me. The thought that I would never again hear his laughter or feel the love that emanated from his eyes, I could not even accept it as real.

We were supposed to have forever. He promised. How could life be so cruel? Maybe Joel really was an angel, sent to save me and show me what love was like only to go back to heaven. Nobody would ever love me the way he did. I would never love anyone the way I loved him. I did not want to fall in love ever again. I couldn't. Joel was my soulmate.

When I pictured the new reality of my future, I saw myself living in our home with Blue, and I'd take care of Peter until he would leave me too. Then I would continue to help the elderly people at his retirement home until I was old myself. I would spend the rest of my life in Peter's cottage, alone. And I'd just wait until I could be reunited with Joel. It was a morbid plan, but at least it was a plan.

Ten days after I said goodbye to Joel, I was released from the hospital. Jeremy had not spoken to me or come to see me since before Joel and I went into surgery. My parents said he just needed time and that he was grieving the only way he knew how. He had already returned to school but had been staying with friends and had not come around much. I missed him. I missed Joel. I missed the way things used to be, even with a sick liver. I still was not able to think very much about the fact that Joel's liver was inside of me. It hurt too much. Part of me had an awareness, and I'd catch myself holding my hand on top of it as if I was protecting it somehow.

My dad came to find me in my room. "Bea, Anna is here to see you."

I panicked. There was no way to avoid this. "Okay."

"Should I send her in? Or do you want me to help you into the living room?"

"You can send her in. Thanks."

I tried to calm my breathing and stop the sick feeling in my stomach from making me throw up. I had loved Anna like a sister.

"Hi," Anna said, standing in my doorway, looking as nervous and sick as I felt.

"Hi, . . . come on in."

Anna stepped inside and approached me where I was propped up in my bed.

"Um, how are you doing? I mean, how's your new liver?" She tried to smile while her eyes glistened with tears.

"It's doing its job, I guess." I could barely look at her. The guilt I felt was eating at me from the inside out. I watched Anna awkwardly stand in front of me, unable to say anything more. I reached for her hand. "Anna, I'm so sorry." I could not stop myself from crying, and the sharp pains in my side were not making it any easier to stop.

Anna continued, "Bea, just let me say what I came to say. I want you to know that my family and I are nothing but grateful to you. You loved my brother in the purest way, and you gave him something that most people never get. Joel fell in love," she wiped her face as she choked on that last word, "with you the day he met you. Every day you were in his life made him the happiest person in the world. I know my brother, and if he had known how things would turn out, he would not have changed a thing. You changed him, made him whole."

"I can't . . . I don't know," I said, trying to control my tears.

"We haven't stayed away from you because we are upset with you," Anna continued. "We are just grieving and still in shock. We have been keeping up to date with your mom, and Cody has been texting me, even though he's pretty sure he's not allowed. My parents wanted me to come over and tell you that you will always be a part of our family, and we love you."

I could not stop crying as tidal waves of relief and love washed over me. I could not say anything, and Anna seemed to understand. Before she left, she handed me an envelope with a beautiful picture of Joel inside. It was an invitation to his celebration of life. I did not stop crying for hours.

I showed up to Joel's celebration of life in his favorite navy-blue sundress, even though it was freezing outside. I had a shawl over my shoulders, and my mom helped me up the driveway and into the house. When I walked in, I was greeted by a table with photos of Joel with his family and many photos of him with me. His ashes were sitting on that table, I knew, yet it still felt like he was just sleeping in that hospital room.

The Petersons had wanted to have a small gathering in their home, where Joel seemed so happy. They greeted me warmly, enveloping me in a loving embrace. Family from California had flown in, and I could recognize some of his relatives by the descriptions he had told me. Joel's mom introduced me to his relatives as the love of Joel's life. I knew they understood the reason Joel died was because his liver was currently inside me, but they were all kind to me. I knew deep down they did not blame me, but the unbelievable guilt was overwhelming.

I stood in the kitchen, looking out the bay window to get a moment alone. I had the celebration's invitation in my hand, and I stared at my love's photo, the tears unable to come as sad as I felt.

"He had a special love for you, Bea." I felt Peter's hand on my shoulder. I turned, and he put his arm around me. I placed my head on his shoulder while I stared at the picture.

"Peter, how could this happen?" I said quietly.

"Bea, you know that Tess and I met much later in life," Peter said. "But I've never told you why."

I turned to look at him, realizing I had never thought about what the reason could have been. I guess I always assumed Peter had been busy building his fortune and working on his career. I always pictured him as a bit of a ladies' man as well.

"I married my high school sweetheart. Her name was Claire. We got married just months after we graduated, much like you and Joel were going to do. Claire was the most beautiful woman I'd ever known. She was so kind, so vibrant, and ten times smarter than I ever was. We moved to England so I could study law, and she went to study linguistics. Three months into our studies, we were on our way to a dinner party when a drunk driver hit us head-on. Claire died instantly."

I stared at Peter. I had been completely unaware that he had this pain he had lived with for most of his long life. He must know exactly how I was feeling.

"Peter, I'm so sorry, I didn't know."

"It's alright, my dear. Because as much as I loved Claire, and I will always love her, life kept going, and I got to meet my beautiful Tess and share so much love and happiness with her."

I stared down at the floor, and he gave me a gentle squeeze. "Darling, your life is only just beginning, and you were so lucky to be sent a love so pure that it even saved your life. Joel would want you to live. He wanted it so badly he was willing to give it up himself."

CHAPTER NINETEEN

‌⸰⸰⸰⸰⸰⸰⸰⸰⸰✕✕✕✕⸰⸰⸰⸰⸰⸰⸰‌

It was mid-January, and I had returned home to Joel's and my place after the Christmas holidays. I could absorb the quiet induced by a blanket of snow surrounding the house, and it was so cozy. It was where so many loving memories had been shared by Joel and me, and by Peter and Tess before us. It was so much fun to watch Blue jump around, eating snow and ice while chasing the squirrels who dared to come out and look for food on his watch. Red cardinals and blue jays happily munched on the nuts I threw out every morning.

Joel's things remained where he had left them. I did not want to touch anything. My mom had come over with Anna yesterday to try and clean things up for me. I knew they had good intentions, but I sent them home instead, insisting that I wanted everything to be left just the way it was. I did not think I was doing anything wrong or unhealthy, which they had suggested. I was not pretending Joel was coming home. I just was not ready to live like he was not. What was wrong with that?

I played Louis Armstrong and Ella Fitzgerald while I ate my meals because that had been Joel's favorite music while he cooked.

I set the table for two, slept on Joel's side of the bed, and wore his favorite Life is Good t-shirt. It still had his scent.

The days and weeks became a blur of sameness. I had no concept of time, and I lived without routine. I did not feel strong enough to venture out of the house, and I did not want to see anyone. I stayed in touch with Jeremy and Anna through text, and I only called my parents in the evening to say goodnight. I also called Peter every few days. I knew he missed me; I knew they all did. I was just not ready to let go yet. Alone in our space without the reality of the outside world, I could spend the day pretending Joel was just at school and that he would be home in a few hours to kiss me and make dinner with me or walk Blue.

I spent the next few weeks thinking about how strange it was that none of us really know one another. We only know what we think we know. This made me wonder about Joel. I wanted to know more about him, his thoughts, his dreams. That is when I remembered his journal.

I frantically searched our bedroom and found it tucked away in the bottom drawer of his nightstand. I carefully removed it and placed it on top of the nightstand, and I sat on his side of the bed to stare at it. Every day for a week, I stood or lay in bed and stared at it, wondering what Joel would think if I opened it and read some of it. I decided to leave it and asked Joel to show me a sign if it was okay.

That sign came a few nights later when I dreamed of Joel. In the dream, Joel was sitting on his side of our bed, where he claimed he got his best ideas. He looked at me and smiled lovingly but did not say anything. Anna walked into the room, holding Jeremy's hand, which was kind of strange, and Joel's parents were laughing at something Blue was doing outside the kitchen window. Everyone was talking and laughing, except for Joel and me. We stared deeply into each other's eyes, and then I suddenly woke up. I realized I felt good and was smiling. It seemed so real, like Joel had visited me in my dreams. I closed my eyes again, hoping to go back into the dream where Joel was.

When I woke up again, I let Blue out, and, after feeding him, I got comfy on the sofa with Blue at my feet, Joel's journal in my hands. I read for a few minutes, savoring every word. I found myself reading his beautifully handwritten sentences over and over, memorizing them. This became my routine every day. I allowed myself two pages a day as I wanted to make it last as long as I could. It made me feel so special, and sometimes his words made me cry with happiness or laugh so hard that Blue looked at me with curiosity. I found myself running my fingers along the pages, following his beautiful cursive, a lost art. I decided I would teach myself how to write in cursive, anything to feel closer to Joel. I added notebooks and pens to my shopping list.

It was two months into my post-surgery healing, and I was feeling pretty good. My scar was ungodly and resembled a Mercedes car emblem. It goes beneath my rib cage on both sides and extends upwards. It is a huge incision. I noticed that I was walking hunched over. This was because my scar was healing well, and as it healed, the skin had begun to shrink. It was gross when I became aware of this, and I had to keep my mind on standing straight, which made the skin stretch in a disgusting way. I wore my scar proudly, though, especially knowing that Joel's beautiful liver was living inside of me. Talk about being close; this was as close as you got.

The medication regime I was on was quite sinister, to say the least. Some of the pills I had to take were like horse pills. There was an insane amount to take each day too. They no longer fit in my checkered bag. One day, when I cleaned it out to discard it for my new blue and green one, which was much more spacious, I had a little breakdown that turned into an all-day crying fest. When I had opened the old bag and dumped the contents out, a small red heart made of paper lay there slightly crumpled and folded in half. I held it in my hands and slowly opened it. It read, "My heart is yours forever." That evening, wearing Joel's pajama bottoms, socks, and one of his hoodies, I decided that tomorrow I would try to rejoin the land of the living.

I awoke to the bright sunshine streaming through the bedroom window. The sky was so blue, almost ice blue. I walked into the kitchen and put on my boots to take Blue outside. It was freezing, and the landscape and trees truly looked like a winter wonderland. The interlocking ice crystals clung to the tree branches in what could only be hoar frost. In some spots, they were so thick that it nearly looked like snow. Even the grass had transformed. The scene was incredible. I suddenly felt sad, thinking about Joel and how he had probably never seen anything like this.

I texted Jeremy with an idea I had. Jeremy was spending more time at home but was very quiet. Joel's death seemed to have affected him on a very deep level. His grief came in waves, and I would catch him staring at me often while I was gaining my strength at my parents' house before I returned to my and Joel's home.

"Why do you keep staring at me?" I had finally asked once.

"I'm not," he replied before getting up and leaving the room.

I had texted him after he left the room.

Bea: *Jer, I miss you. Please talk to me, or text me at least. Xo*

Jer: *Bea, just give me some time, okay?*

Bea: *I get that, but why can't you be around me?*

Jer: *Bea.*

I heard Jeremy's steps coming toward my room. He knocked.

"Come in."

"Bea, . . . when I look at you, all I can think about is how I ruined your life by not being the one who donated," he said through glossy eyes. I had never really seen my brother cry before. "I was a match too. I should never have let Joel go through with it. I'm your brother, for God's sake." He hung his head down low, covering his face with his hands.

"Jer," I began. That was all I had the chance to say before he turned and left.

Wow, at least now I understood a little better. It was survivor's guilt, I believed. Cody had given me a pamphlet along with a good luck card before I left the hospital. He strongly urged me to read it, which I had been grateful for. As it turned out, survivor's guilt was a very real thing and happened to people who go through a stage of believing they had actually done something wrong by surviving a traumatic event when others did not, which creates a lot of self-guilt.

I had experienced it at the beginning, but then I would recall what Joel had said to me before we had the operation. He had said, "This is our battle, and we'll fight it together." That stuck with me as I battled my feelings of guilt, knowing that Joel had thought about it and had chosen to do such an amazing thing for me. I decided I would feel guiltier not appreciating what Joel had sacrificed for me. It was weird, but I felt his presence like he was with me. I wanted to make him proud of me and to know that I had not taken his gift in vain. I would keep working on Jeremy, one day at a time.

Just as I had been replaying this memory in my mind, I heard Jeremy's car in the driveway and then the crunching of the frost and snow as he walked up the path. I got up and walked toward the front door where my brother was standing with Peter at his side, ready to offer him a hand.

"Hey, Sis, nice to see you." It was so good to see my brother smiling down at me, if only for a second.

"You look terrible, Jer!" We both laughed as we exchanged our normal brother-sister banter.

"Hello, young lady!" Peter said as he carefully came into the house with Jeremy's help.

I kissed him on the cheek, which was wet with cold. "Peter, you're a sight for sore eyes. Welcome!"

Peter looked around, a curious look on his face. I bet it must have been strange standing in his old home. He smiled and pointed at the pictures on the walls. "Those are the same pictures that have been on those ancient walls for years! My God, do you ever have terrible taste, sweet Bea!" The three of us laughed.

"Jeremy, would you like to stay for some coffee or something?"

"No thanks, I don't want to die today." Jeremy used to always say things like that whenever I was cooking or making something in the kitchen. Today, our new reality without Joel in it came crashing down on us in that one moment. "Sorry, I didn't mean . . . ."

"It's okay, Jer. Why don't you come back for Peter in an hour or so? Okay?" I gave him a small hug.

"Yeah, sure, sounds good. Peter, don't let her do anything more than sit down, okay?"

"No problem, son. As luck would have it, I know my way around this kitchen already. Beatrice, please take a seat in the parlor while I make us some coffee."

It felt so good to be with Peter. If only Joel could have been here with us. We had been so excited about our wedding and wanted to show Peter and Tess all the changes we had made, along with all the things we had left alone to remind us of them.

"Bea, how are things going with your brother? It seems he's taking things rather hard," Peter said as he rummaged around the kitchen. "He didn't speak much on the way here."

"Yeah, I have tried talking to him many times, but he only opened up to me for a moment, and that was it. He says he ruined my and Joel's lives because he should have been the one to step up to the plate and offer me his liver."

"I see," Peter said with sadness on his sweet face. "It must be hard, especially after Joel asked him to be his best man. They were pretty close, weren't they?"

It took me a moment to process what Peter had just said. "I didn't know about that," I said. With Joel, Jeremy and Anna all going to school and my illness, we really had not spent too much time talking about the details of our wedding. We seemed to care mostly about the actual getting married and living happily ever after part, more than the wedding itself.

"It behooves me to have been the one to let that slip," Peter continued as he poured hot water into the coffee machine. "But I thought you should know that when you were unwell, Jeremy and Joel spent a lot of time together. I believe they had been much closer than you'd previously known, my dear girl."

Peter looked sorrowful as he took my hand in his. We talked about Tess and his health, and Peter even tried to tell me a joke but stopped right in the middle, sensing that I was not quite there yet.

"Silly old Peter and his jokes! Would you like to hear something you haven't heard already?" Peter said, sitting up taller, with excitement and love filling his eyes.

"Okay, you've got my attention. Let's hear it. As long as it's not a joke."

"I promise." He carefully sat in one of the dining chairs beside me and handed me one of the mugs in his hand. I knew there were almond milk and two pumps of honey in mine, just the way I liked it. "Did you know that Joel was writing a book?"

"Well, yeah, he was always writing something, you know that."

"Yes, he sure was, wasn't he," Peter chuckled. "Joel's writing style was truly original. He might have had a brilliant career, Bea."

Peter looked up at me directly, as if to make sure I had heard him. He continued, "Joel called me the night you were in the hospital together before the operation. You were asleep. He told me that Anna was going to give me an envelope in the morning." Peter opened up his sweater and took a thick envelope out of his inside pocket. He looked at it appreciatively before handing it to me.

"What's this?"

"That, my dear Bea, is Joel's manuscript. He had finished it and wanted me to read it before he gave it to you on your wedding day. It was his gift to you. It is quite good, and I wanted to wait until you were stronger before giving it to you. I hope you aren't cross that I'd held on to it so long."

"Oh my gosh, Peter." My heart felt happy for the first time in so long as I took the envelope from his hands and clutched it. "This is amazing!" I leaned in and hugged him. "Wow! This is, well, it is a special gift. I'm so glad he finished it." I clutched the envelope to my chest, as my tears were absorbed into the paper that Joel had held in his beautiful hands.

After Jeremy had helped Peter back into his car, he ran back to give me a hug. A real hug. "Let me know when you're up for another visitor." He smiled.

"I will, and Jeremy?"

"Yeah?"

"I love you."

"Love you too."

CHAPTER TWENTY

For the next few weeks, I devoured every word of Joel's book. It was so incredible knowing that he'd come up with the ideas, the characters, the thoughts, and feelings that were written on each page. It was as though he were right there beside me telling the story.

It was a fiction romance novel. I was pretty sure the main characters were based on the two of us, which really made me smile. He wrote in a way that inspired readers to submerge themselves into the world that he had created, letting time and space fall away.

I had also continued reading Joel's journal, the one I'd given him last Christmas. I was nearly to his last entry, and I felt sick at the thought of coming to the end of his words. I began thinking about Joel telling me that he had been journaling ever since he could read and write. I instantly became obsessed with the thought of reading more of his words, learning everything I could about this person I loved so much. Every new thing that I learned about him was a new treasure I could bury deep into my subconscious mind, where nobody would ever find it or take it away. I would have a treasure trove of memories, which would become my most valuable collection.

The winter was not usually my favorite season because it was the coldest time of the year, bringing freezing temperatures, snow, and ice. This year, however, I felt like it was the perfect weather for how I was feeling. I was stronger, that was for sure. I had even begun doing short workouts in my bedroom with a few light weights I'd found in the garage one day. Mostly, though, I felt exactly like the ice outside—frozen.

The only time I felt warm was when I was reading Joel's words and when I could pretend he was right there with me. Of course, I loved talking to Peter, and I called my parents on the phone every day, but I didn't really want to talk to anyone. I just wanted to be alone with my thoughts and with Joel's words.

I was aware that I needed something more, but I had absolutely no idea what to do about this. I knew I was being super hard on myself; I mean, I just had a liver transplant. Dr. Cooper said that it takes three months before a person feels somewhat strong enough to begin some type of routine or have some semblance of a life. It takes six months until a person is fully functioning and pain-free.

The glaring problem for me was that most of my pain had nothing to do with my liver, at least not directly. My pain came from what my liver had taken away from me. My pain was ice cold and created an empty void inside of me that left me numb and feeling like time stood still.

I had some ideas of what I could be doing, such as contacting Crystal, the manager of Peter's retirement home, and getting a volunteer schedule approved for the coming months. I could maybe even apply to college to pursue my scholastic goals. However, neither of those goals made me feel anything.

Recently, I'd become curious about the idea of becoming a doctor, maybe even a liver specialist, like Dr. Cooper, but it seemed like a lot of time to invest. Of course, I would be able to help a lot of people. But I wanted to do something that mattered now.

Peter has a beautiful hourglass with sand inside called a sand timer. It had a sleek gold finish to the slender metal sides, giving it a hint of glamor, with brown-finished wooden accents to warm up the look. Peter liked to remind me while I visited that the only time that is important is now. He'd turn the glass over, and after a few moments, cover the top so you could not see how much sand was left, and he'd point to the narrowed middle that allows a small amount of the sand through. He would point to that narrow spot and very seriously say, "Right there is the place you should be living—in the present."

I didn't really get that until recently. And that is why I knew that school was not the immediate answer.

Joel used to tell me that he had known he wanted to be a writer his entire life, ever since he could remember. That wasn't the same for me. I used to want to be a reporter, travelling the world, going wherever there was excitement and danger. But then I got sick, and everything changed. I learned that life was fragile and that there were many people suffering. I decided that I wanted to help others. I just needed to figure out what way to do so.

So many things are different for me now. I could go anywhere in the world that I want. No longer did I have to worry about healthcare, travel insurance, or being away from my family out of fear. I began to scour the internet for ideas on things I could do with my life that would make sense. I felt that the right thing would show up, and I would suddenly just know, just like I had when I met Joel.

People say that there are no coincidences in life and that people and opportunities show up when you are ready. Well, I wanted to let the universe know that I was ready, and what better way to get out there than to surf the world wide web. I would spend the lion's share of my days jumping back and forth from reading Joel's words to walking Blue, jumping back on the computer search engines and typing in everything I could think of that related to volunteering, and then back to reading Joel's words. Each day that I grew closer to that final entry, another knot tied itself up in my stomach.

One day, while I was doing a deep dive into a green peace organization, an ad popped up about alcohol. It was a warning of the effects of alcohol on the liver and was sponsored by the Liver Foundation. An idea began to take root in my mind, and I quickly sent an email to the foundation and pressed send just as the doorbell rang.

"Hello!" A cheery voice I recognized came from the front of the house, as she let herself in, with the door closing loudly and Blue barking with excitement.

I called out, "In here, Anna."

I had not seen Anna for a few weeks now, but we had been staying in touch every day by text. She was also keeping me posted on how her parents were doing. They had both taken some time off work and had gone on a seven-day cruise in Greece. Anna had said that they were trying to get closer and felt this would be a necessary, albeit temporary, distraction from the emptiness they felt without Joel.

"Hi there, lovely!" Anna came into the room. She looked great, her long brown hair tied behind her in a cute ponytail. I was grateful that Anna looked and acted so different from her brother. It would be so hard otherwise. Although they had similar features and coloring, Anna had blue eyes and freckles. She was also very outgoing and outwardly cheerful. Joel had green eyes and was as introverted as Anna was extroverted. The two of them, when together, had made for an interesting study of opposites.

"How are you feeling?" Anna asked.

"I'm feeling good," I replied honestly. "Nice surprise seeing you."

"Did you forget? We were going to go through some of Joel's boxes, the ones he hadn't unpacked yet. I'd love to help. I thought it might be nice for you to have some more of his things around. Do you feel up for that?"

"To be honest, I knew you were coming over this morning, but I lost track of time somewhere along the way."

"No problem. I can come back another time. What were you doing?"

"No, now is great, Anna. I'm really glad you're here." I got up and walked over to give her a hug. "I've missed you."

"Missed me? We text a hundred times a day."

"I don't have many people in my life. My parents, Peter, Jeremy, and you, that's it. But I like it that way, to be honest."

"Well, I know the feeling."

"What happened to Eric?"

"Eric is great, but I just needed a bit of space. He has been a great friend, but he's not the one. Not very many people our age find what you and Joel had."

"No, they don't. I do consider myself one of the lucky ones."

Anna opened her mouth to speak but then closed it.

"What?" I asked.

"Nothing, it's just something Joel used to say when we were kids."

"Tell me," I said.

As she spoke, she wore pain on her face through her distant smile. "Joel used to always correct everyone when they'd say they were lucky."

"What do you mean, correct?"

"He'd say, 'You're not lucky, Anna. You're blessed.' And he would always say that, to anyone, if they dared to say they were lucky."

I smiled, imagining the little boy I had seen in pictures, wearing a Mickey Mouse sweater and always carrying a book. "That's very wise for a little boy."

"He was a weird kid. I never knew where he got that from. But it went on for years."

We both regarded one another sadly, with no words needed to share our pain.

"Let me get my coat, and we can bring the boxes into the living room," I told Anna.

We unloaded six boxes from Anna's car and carried them inside.

"I'll make a pot of peach tea, okay?" I said.

"Sure. I'll play with Blue while you make the tea." Anna grabbed a nearby toy and started playing with him.

Once we were settled on the living room floor, we began to empty the boxes with the precious contents of Joel's life. There were mostly books, clothes, and a couple of bottles of his favorite colognes. I wanted it all but wanted to let Anna choose what she wanted to keep.

"Anna, why don't you fill up this box with whatever you want to keep."

"That is sweet of you, Bea. Joel left behind a bunch of things in his room. This is all yours unless you don't want something. I don't want to get rid of any of it, so I'll take whatever you don't want."

Anna got busy folding some of Joel's clothes. She held a sweater up to her face and looked like she was about to cry.

"Oh my gosh. Look." Anna pointed to the box she was empty-ing and stacked in a neat pile were a bunch of journals. "Joel's journals. I had forgotten about those. I gave him that one right there." She pointed to a navy-blue leather-bound journal.

"He loved that thing." She smiled, remembering precious moments with her brother. I thought about what it would be like if I lost Jeremy, and I honestly could not imagine it. And Joel was her twin, so that must be even harder.

"Do you want to keep those, Anna?"

"Absolutely not. Those should stay with you. I bet Joel would want you to read them, to get some insight into more of his life." Anna stopped talking and leaned forward to retrieve the journal at the top. She gently opened the journal and found a little dried up yellow flower. "What's this?"

I gasped. "Can I see that?"

Anna handed me the tan-colored journal with gold flecks, opened to where the little flower had been placed with care. I looked at the date on the journal entry and realized it was the first day we had met. It read, *September 13, I met a girl today whose eyes challenge the blue of the ocean. They could replace it altogether. The beauty of the ocean has a new name for me. Bea.*

"I can't believe it. It's the flower I gave him when we first met after he'd fallen off his skateboard. I can't believe he kept it." I thought back to that amazing day, the first day of the rest of my life, the day I had fallen in love with the most beautiful soul on the planet.

"I knew he was sentimental, but wow." Anna smiled. "You definitely should read those. I bet you'll get a few laughs and cries out of them."

"Don't you think they should be left alone and kept private?"

"No way! I knew my brother. He would want you to read them. In fact, I am going to let myself out and leave you alone to do just that. I know you're dying to." Anna smiled lovingly.

I stared at Joel's journals for many moments after Anna left. I read well into the night until I finished the journal with the flower. I fell asleep dreaming of Joel. When I woke up, I had a knowing feeling, a feeling that everything would be okay. I realized, fully, that Joel coming into my life was the best gift in the world, and I was not going to waste it. I placed my hand lovingly over the place where my new liver thrived and said a silent thank you.

I went for my morning walk with Blue and then settled myself at the kitchen table in Joel's spot, flicked open my computer, and checked my emails with a feeling of hope and excitement.

In my inbox was the email I'd been hoping to see. It was from Jason Hendrick, the president of the Liver Foundation. I excitedly opened it and read, "Dear Beatrice, It would be an honor to meet with you and discuss having you as an Ambassador for the National Liver Foundation. In addition, we would like to invite you to speak and share your story with us for our annual Liver Gala this spring. We truly are grateful for you contacting us and look forward to a long relationship. Please contact me to arrange a meeting with me and the board. Sincerely, Jason Hendrick, President of the National Liver Foundation.

This was it. This was what I was meant to do. Be a spokesperson for the Liver Foundation and bring awareness to liver disease. I wanted to help people with autoimmune hepatitis and their families. I'd always loved public speaking and wanted to share my story and the love that Joel and I shared with the world.

One Saturday morning, I sat with Peter in front of the pond at my house. Blue played and chased the squirrels as they started to come out of hiding with the promise of a new season on the way.

"Peter, what if I submitted Joel's book to some publishers? I really think someone would pick it up," I said as I looked out at the brilliant sunlight reflecting off the frozen water.

"Bea, I think that is the best idea you've had in a long time, next to your idea to contact the Liver Foundation, that is. Joel talked of doing just that."

"Really? Why didn't you say so before?"

"I knew you'd think of it on your own, dear."

That night I decided it was time to read the last journal entries Joel had written before he died. With shaking hands, I climbed into his side of our bed, wearing his clothes, and opened the journal to the last few pages. I realized there was only one entry left. These were Joel's final thoughts, the last words he ever wrote, the last I'd ever read. It was dated the day before I went into the hospital. My whole body shook, and I fought the urge to cry. With a deep breath, I clutched the little book and gathered all my strength to read these last few words.

The page read, *When I met Bea, I realized I would be with her for the rest of my life. Every day that I get with her will be a gift from this day forward. We never know when our lives might change forever, and often it happens in the blink of an eye. Yesterday is in the past, tomorrow isn't promised, but forever is today.*

CHAPTER TWENTY-ONE

⬥⬥⬥⬥⬥

It was the early days of May, and the last couple of months had been filled with excitement and renewed hope for the future as I filled my days doing things that felt meaningful. Of course, there was never a moment without the feeling of deep longing as I lived with an emptiness in my life that would never fully go away. I made it a daily ritual to read Joel's journals and learn more about who he was. It was truly a blessing, and each day began and ended with the gift of his words.

I had gone to New York City several times to meet with Jason Hendrick from the Liver Association. He was a kind man with a genuine desire to make a difference in this world and for those who suffer from my illness. I had learned that he had lost his son to liver disease a few years ago when he was only thirteen years old.

When I shared my story with him and the other board members, there was not a dry eye in the room. They decided that we would record my story and place it on the national website for the world to hear. This made me feel much braver than I thought possible. The rest of the board consisted of members who all had been affected by liver disease. We all had a story; we had all lost someone or feared it every day. By the end of spring, I had gotten to know so many strong men, women, and children, who one day may need to go through the same thing I did.

One Saturday morning, I took the train down to the city to meet with Mr. Hendrick. The return of the birds and the buds on the trees in Central Park brought the excitement of a new chapter, one that I knew would change my life forever. I walked briskly with a new energy I had never known in my entire lifetime. For the first time, I felt not only healthy, but I felt alive. I felt a sense of deep purpose every day because I had something important to share with the world.

My and Joel's story was my deepest heartbreak, my salvation, and my reason for living. He had not only loved me, changed me, and saved me, but he had helped me find myself. He had given my life a greater meaning than I ever thought I would know. Every day for the rest of my life, his love and strength would be there with me, holding me together.

I arrived at the little French bistro, where I was meeting Jason Hendrick. I saw him as soon as I walked in, and he smiled at me warmly.

"Hello, Bea," he said as I came up to the table.

"Hey Jason," I said cheerfully.

He stood and helped me with my coat, placing it on the back of my chair. He pushed my chair in and sat back down in the chair opposite.

A waitress came up to the table. "Welcome, can I get you folks some drinks to start? It's happy hour currently, so we have some excellent wines available at five dollars a glass."

I looked at Jason, who smiled knowingly at me.

"We'll take two sparkling waters with lemon, please," he said to the server. He handed her the drink menu. "We won't be needing this."

"Alright, coming right up." The woman said, taking the menu from his waiting hand.

"You look radiant today, Bea," Jason said.

"I feel good. Getting stronger every day." I gave him a big smile.

"So, what is the purpose of our meeting today, my dear," he said. "You sounded so excited over the phone."

"I feel as though everything in my life has happened for a reason. It took some time for that reason to be revealed, but it did come. I realize that while the way things have played out has caused so much pain for me and my loved ones, it will be able to bring so much hope to thousands of others."

"I know that you have suffered a great ordeal, but let me just say how lucky we feel to have you working with us now."

"We're not lucky," I said. "We're blessed. And I was blessed with knowing an incredible person, someone who will continue to change the world even now that he's gone."

I reached into my bag and pulled out a small piece of folded paper. "I got Joel's book published. It's coming out next summer," I said. "And he and I would like to donate all the royalties to the Liver Foundation, from now until forever."

I handed Jason the first check from the publishing company, written out to the National Liver Foundation.

Jason stared at me and slowly took the folded check. He opened it and stared at the amount in shock. Tears welled up in his silver-blue eyes.

"Bea, this . . . ," he stammered. "This is incredible."

"It's what Joel would have wanted."

"I don't know what to say."

"Say that you will use this money to change lives. And promise me that we will keep working on finding a cure."

"I promise." Jason got up, and I followed. He hugged me tightly, patting me on the back. "Thank you so much."

He let go, and we sat back down. "I'm not much of a fiction reader, but I will definitely be reading this book. What's it called, by the way?"

I smiled at him warmly, as if I could feel Joel next to me. "It's called *Forever is Today*."

Epilogue

From as far back as I can remember, I've loved words and the way no other art form expresses an idea quite the same. Words create worlds within your mind, they pull emotions from within you, and they make you think about what you have just read for days, weeks, or a lifetime.

When you master words and the ability to weave them together just so, you become a creator. You create a world that starts with one silent idea inside your mind, which then expands into people, with friends, families, and interests. And then you give them a story of their own. The goal is always to share your work, get it published, and when you do, you will have succeeded at creating an entire universe that becomes alive in the minds of millions.

I have spent my whole life thinking about what makes a work of written words important and memorable. I have come to believe that the works that have stood the test of time all shared a common goal—to make one experience a range of emotions. The beauty of words is like no other form of art in that writing can richly capture a person's deepest desire, pain, fear, or joy. Other kinds of artwork can only suggest these emotions.

Writers enjoy a certain extra freedom when creating. We are not bound by a limited number of notes to form a melody like musicians. We do not have to make do with the existing world like photographers. And I think that our literary masterpieces are better understood than the works of visual artists, who have to leave their works to the viewer's own imagination.

With the ability to use almost limitless combinations of words, I like to think writers have "more brushes and more colors of paint" than any artist. We can create images with colors that do not exist, while our characters are free to develop into exactly who they want to be.

On a special night of the year, where words are celebrated at an event in New York City, I found myself for the first time without any words. With a glass of champagne in one hand and feeling short of breath no matter how much I loosened my tie, I knew this night would change my and my family's lives forever.

I watched the evening commencing as people made their way to their tables, and the opening jazz musicians packed up their instruments. I made my way to my table, greeting some of the individuals being honored who were sitting with me. With a smile in my heart, I waited for the event to start. After the guests were seated, everyone hushed as our host for the evening walked up on stage. He reached the podium and spoke into the microphone.

"Welcome to the Annual Fiction Writers of America Awards!"

The room erupted into applause and cheering.

"As we begin our evening, I'd like to say a few words about the men and women we are honoring," the host continued, looking around the room at our smiling faces full of anticipation.

"They say that more than 80 percent of Americans would like to be an author, but the percentage of those who actually finish writing a book are far fewer. It is estimated that 329,259 books were published in the United States this year alone, while 2.2 million books were published around the world. Over 130 million books have been published in human history. It might seem improbable to finish a book, let alone have it stand the test of time with true literary merit. The authors we are honoring tonight are not just the creators of our favorite characters, but they are the voices of our generation. For the words they have so kindly woven together for our reading pleasure will shape the thoughts of the young and old for years to come. These writers have left an imprint of today's world on the world of tomorrow. And without further ado, I have the privilege of announcing the winners of the Annual Fiction Writers of America Awards."

The host held up an envelope in his hand, and the crowd cheered again.

"For our first award tonight for the best romantic fiction novel, it's not every day you come across a work that has inspired so much love in the world. A great love story is hard to come by these days, and it is always a welcomed reminder that however rare, true love prevails. Ladies and gentlemen, the winner of the Fiction Writers of America Award for romantic fiction is . . . Joel Emmet Peterson."

The crowd erupted, and I smiled as my image flashed across the giant monitors on either side of the stage and stood to receive my award. My beautiful wife, Bea, stood as well and jumped into my arms as everyone watched. I kissed her and twirled her around as the crowd continued to applaud.

"We did it," I whispered to her.

"You did it," she whispered back and laughed with joy. I left her at the table and walked up the steps to the center stage. Our host handed me my award and left me standing at the podium, the entire room waiting for what I had to say.

"Thank you for this incredible award for a book that is dear to me. It's a rare opportunity to find someone who makes your life so worthwhile that you're willing to die for them. For those of you who read my book, *Forever is Today*, you know that the ending is bittersweet. Yes, I wrote this book based on the true story of myself and my beloved wife, Bea, to whom I gave 60 percent of my liver just weeks before our wedding. I am happy to say that I made it through the surgery, and therefore was able to write the heartbreak that almost happened to us in the form of this fictional book. I did have an allergic reaction to the anesthesia, and I went into a coma for three days. In those three days, I saw many visions in the form of dreams. These visions were of the love of my life trying to live without me, and I captured this heartbreak in the last chapters of this book. I was inspired to write them because, in the state of my coma, they did happen. And I knew that I had to wake up, for Bea, for my family, and for this book to help thousands of others suffering from autoimmune hepatitis. Bea, this book is a tribute to you and my love for your beautiful spirit. I truly mean it when I say, 'Forever is today and every day that I love you.'"

ABOUT THE AUTHOR

Author, speaker, mindset expert, and professional risk-taker, Janet-Lynn Morrison is a writer who might take you to the edge of a heart-stopping cliff or to the point of falling into the deepest love. Or, maybe a bit of both.

Janet-Lynn carries one fundamental belief with her everywhere she goes. It's the reason she's been able to experience the highest and lowest points of life, how she's come to understand the power of love, and why you're holding this book right now. She believes in *living impossibly*. When you live life without limits, the impossible starts to occur. And it all starts in the mind.

Janet-Lynn now invites you to read the story of her daughter, Maddy Rose, the inspiration for Bea in *Forever is Today,* to learn more about how a modern young woman lives with autoimmune hepatitis.

My Name is Maddy Rose

M y name is Maddy Rose, and I am twenty years old. Five years ago, I lay on my bed at The Hospital for Sick Kids (SickKids) in Toronto, where I was diagnosed with a rare form of liver disease known as autoimmune hepatitis type 1. To briefly explain, autoimmune disease is where one's immune system is triggered by either a genetic predisposition or an environmental factor, and instead of attacking and killing harmful bacteria or viruses that sneak into your body (such as a cold virus), your immune system actually begins to try to get rid of things that are supposed to be in your body.

In my case, my immune system is attacking my liver. This is a big problem as your liver is the second biggest organ in your body and is in charge of performing over 500 essential tasks that are key to keeping your body healthy and functioning. Liver disease is often referred to as the silent killer as symptoms can be difficult to spot. It is only when your liver is already in serious trouble that symptoms become more prominent.

Prior to receiving my diagnosis, I distinctly recall the symptoms of liver failure I experienced but didn't understand at the time. I remember losing interest in life. I had always enjoyed and done well in school, yet suddenly I found myself not doing my homework or concentrating in class. A wall slowly formed between my friends and me, and I never wanted to do anything anymore, and no one understood why. All of the hobbies I had come to enjoy seemed to fade away as the only thing I could bring myself to do was watch TV.

I was so tired *all* of the time to the point where I would fall asleep during a fifteen-minute car ride, skip class to lay my head down in the library, and I couldn't bring myself to participate in any of my usual afterschool activities. Eventually, I even lost interest in eating as it just required too much energy. It wasn't until I began to turn yellow that alarm bells started to go off. Teachers and classmates began commenting, and my family became extremely worried as I slowly transformed from Maddy, the fifteen-year-old girl, to Maddy, the walking banana.

The day I walked into the emergency room of my local hospital was the day that my life changed forever. The doctor on call declared that he was shocked that I hadn't come in sooner as my blood work was showing some alarming results. I was admitted to the pediatric division of the hospital that night. After a few days, numerous tests and too many needles to count, the doctor watching over me admitted that they didn't have the tests available to find out why I was so sick and that I was going to be transferred to The Hospital for Sick Kids in Toronto.

Honestly, I was pretty out of it at this point but remembered a long ride to the city and arriving at this new hospital in the middle of the night where I was greeted by the staff like an old friend and shown to the room in which I would be staying for the next month. Within the first night at SickKids, the doctors on my case already had an idea of my diagnosis. The game plan moving forward was to try and implement an extensive enough regimen of medication to pull my liver back from the point of needing a transplant.

In between tests and procedures, I actually have fond memories of my stay at SickKids. I was lucky enough to have met many of the hospital's dogs and three NHL Maple Leaf hockey players. I had access to a delicious menu with all of my favorite foods, stacks of games, crafts, and books brought to me by family and friends. I received get-well cards from my classmates at school and made some new friends with the volunteers who graciously offered their time to keep me company. When I was well enough, I even got to see an amazing Christmas play downtown with my family, courtesy of the hospital. Looking back, I am so incredibly grateful and thankful for the pure love and care I received during my stay.

I was finally allowed to go home only a couple of days before Christmas and was welcomed home with a slobbery kiss from my one-eyed dog Mandy whom I had missed so much. It was during this time that a new battle began.

My new life heavily revolved around dealing with medication side effects. The side effects I endured ranged from rashes and hair loss to raging and uncontrollable appetite, to nightmares and sleepless nights altogether. Not to mention having loom over me the possible long-term side effects of bone cancer, skin cancer, developing another autoimmune disease, and ultimately needing a liver transplant one day.

During my recovery, I was only at school for a couple of half days a week, and when I wasn't at school, I was sitting in my bedroom staring at the wall. I found myself wondering how my life had changed so drastically in what seemed like such a short period of time. I felt lost, alone, and as if I had no control over my own life. It's a pretty scary thing to think you're fine and healthy one day just to find out you are at death's door the next. What was going to happen to all of my future plans? How can I go to university when I hardly have the energy to make it until lunchtime? How can I travel the world when I can't go longer than two weeks without seeing a doctor? How will I ever move forward when it seems like every day there's yet another mountain to climb?

Now, five years later, I am so excited to share that Gilbert (yes, I named my liver) and I are feeling the best we have in a long time. I have been transferred to Toronto General Hospital, where I am in the care of some of the most brilliant doctors in the country. I am currently on the lowest doses of my medications that I have been on since I was diagnosed. I have traveled to Australia and Europe and even spent one summer doing a cross-Canada adventure by train!

After years of struggle, I am finally feeling back to my normal self. Of course, I have limitations and things I have to be cautious of that the average person doesn't have to worry about. But when reflecting on the journey I had to endure to get from where I was to where I am today, I realize that I have grown as a person in more ways than I would have ever thought imaginable.

I am able to live in the moment and enjoy the little things so much more because I have experienced firsthand that even the little things are a tremendous gift to us. We never know when our lives might change forever, and often it happens in the blink of an eye. Yesterday is in the past, tomorrow isn't promised, but forever is today.

HEARTS to be HEARD

Giving a Voice to Creativity!

With every donation, a voice will be given to the creativity that lies within the hearts of our children living with diverse challenges.

By making this difference, children that may not have been given the opportunity to have their Heart Heard will have the freedom to create beautiful works of art and musical creations.

Donate by visiting

HeartstobeHeard.com

We thank you.